THE GARDEN

The Kingdom of Enneahedral Series

Book 5

K. S. CAROL

World Castle Publishing, LLC
Pensacola, Florida

Copyright © K. S. Carol 2015
Print ISBN: 9781629894034
eBook ISBN: 9781629894041
First Edition World Castle Publishing, LLC, October 28, 2015
http://www.worldcastlepublishing.com

Cover: Paul Barton II
Editor: Chrissy Szarek

CHAPTER 1

The cold was seeping into her bones. Not only that, but Aurora thought maybe her body would never be warm again. Or clean. There wasn't a drop of water warm enough to bathe in either. But Trianam told her that soon, soon it would be over and the sun would warm them again. She hoped so. He'd been telling her that for days now and they didn't have any kind of break in the weather. And it had been too long, in her estimation. Too long for the sun to tell the trees that it was time.

"There is a melting in the field to our left."

She looked in the direction that Markard was pointing.

"I saw grasses sprouting up. Mayhap we should move to that area. 'Tis warmer."

"Thank goodness." Aurora picked up the journal she'd been making notes in and shoved it into the satchel she carried. "I know that we've only been here for a few weeks, but I want to feel the warmth on my face again."

Markard nodded and went back to his wagon. She had no idea what he was making today but he'd been up since before she had been. He and Vildar had been working nonstop for the three days that they'd been waiting for the thaw. She was glad they were keeping busy, but she was bored too and wanted something to do, even if she had no idea how to work with them.

"I've a notion to speak with you." Trianam's voice caught her attention.

Aurora nodded, almost afraid to hear what Trianam had to tell her now.

"Did you know that the trees have started to bloom in the wagon? I've told the man thrice now that he keeps it too warm. Now we've a stand of trees and no earth to plant them in. What will we do with them once they start to bear fruit? Hope we can eat it all before they die off too."

"You said it would be soon. You've been saying that to us for days now. It'll be soon. I swear to you if you say that to me again I'm going to run you through. And Markard just told me that he saw some grass sprouting." Aurora took a deep breath. They'd been snapping and biting at each other, all of them, since they arrived. Taking another deep breath, she tried to think reasonably but Trianam started barking at her again.

"You'll tell him he's to stop keeping the place so heated up that nothing has a chance but to grow too large. Nothing I say to him works. It's as though I'm speaking to a child. Nay, like I would be talking to the snow."

Aurora opened her mouth to tell him to do it himself, when she took a step back. It wasn't just her, she thought, something was affecting them all. When Trianam stepped toward her she put up her hand. He stopped.

"This isn't us." He frowned at her. "We talk, we work things out, but we don't bite at each other like mortal enemies. Something is doing this. I don't want to argue with you anymore. Something is messing with our heads."

He looked around the fields they were in, and she could see that he was thinking about what she'd said.

His neck popped several times, and she knew that he was fighting with himself as hard as she was. "We're being made to fight and argue. Working against each other instead of together like we usually do. And I'm sorry to say this, but it's getting harder and harder not to run you through."

"Aye, I've felt the same about you. And it matters little how small the problem or that I can more than likely solve it meself. I want to murder you." He looked around again, this time with his hand on his sword. "I'm afear that it's nothing we can fight with nary a sword. There is blackness in my heart where there was none before this."

That was a good description of what she was feeling. A dark pall had befallen them, and she hated it.

"Bring the others here. We have to figure this out before we kill each other. And as I have things to finish up here, I don't think that's such a good idea." Trianam walked away.

She closed her eyes. Reaching into the air around her, Aurora tried to find what it was when something touched her mind.

"'Tis not you, my lady."

She looked around for the source, and heard the voice again.

"I can't but stay here for a bit. The cold will harm me, and I've no wish to be murdered."

It was then that she realized it wasn't someone small and here with her. Aurora knelt down to look at the blades of grass. The snow around it had been trampled a little but the small greenery had been left alone. She touched one of the blades and felt its weakness.

"Tell me what it is you need to then go below the ground. I wish to know what is making us feel this way, but not enough to have you harmed. Hurry."

The small blade nodded and spoke quickly. "The winter air has decided it's here to stay. He hates that he only had two months to cover the earth when the sun has all year. The sun refuses to melt it, because the earth said it won't accept the warmth it gives us because he is tired of the snow getting his way. He claims that the snow has been tainted and it will kill all who drink from it. We have been hidden beneath the earth for so long now we fear that we may never return. The king of here, he has made it so we are forever hidden away."

Aurora sat down. "You mean, this is here to stay? That there will be no melting of the snow because of jealousy? That is the most ridicules thing I've ever heard. And who is the supposed king? Last I heard, there was no one but the one that sits in his mountain."

The little green leaves nodded to her.

"What do you know of the time of year? Are we indeed approaching the summer months or the beginning of winter?"

"It's a new season, my lady. One we will all miss again if this is not taken care of." The little leaves seemed to stand up straighter. "I didn't mean to say you aren't doing your job, my lady champion. I only meant to say that...well, we have been like this for many seasons. I fear this one will be no different, if we aren't helped. You will help us, will you not?" The tiny greens seemed to shiver again and then disappeared.

Aurora was still sitting there trying to figure out why this made them angry all the time when Zapps sat beside her.

"You'll get a cold where no medicine can help you," he said.

She looked at him, thinking that the man was entirely too happy to have been in the cold for this long without any sign of relief. Of all the people with her, she just realized that Zapps and his cousin, Tholan, hadn't been affected. "You do know that it's not possible to get a cold in your butt, right?" Aurora quipped. He laughed. "You and Tholan, you're not affected by the war going on between us, are you? I've only just realized that you and he aren't snapping and biting at each other."

"War, my lady?" He looked around the fields then back at her. "I know not of a war unless you mean the one between you and Trianam and the other band of merry men. He is fairly frothing at the mouth at something you did. But then you were angry with him as well if memory serves. But nay, we aren't fighting with you, as you have said."

"I didn't do anything to Trianam. He's just..." She felt the anger surge forward and snapped her mouth closed until she could get a better grip on it. "I just spoke to the grass. She said that the snow and the sun are fighting over the melting of this stuff. Apparently the snow has covered this part of the world for a good long time and he's claimed that it's poisoned. The sun is holding off melting it because of that. And there is this king I've yet to meet. How many kings are there, anyway? And it's been so long, they fear that everything here might all die, they're in a sort of limbo. But I don't know that if he melts it, it won't, anyway."

"Just the one king, the dragon king. And I thought it was close to the melting."

She shook her head.

"That would explain a good deal. I was walking with one of the wings when he mentioned that the snow has not fallen in the time we've been here, yet it doesn't seem to melt by the sun of the day. Why would they bicker so?"

"I don't know, but until we figure this out, we're going to be cold." She stood up and brushed the snow off her legs.

Zapps simply shook his great body and the snow flew off.

Aurora smiled. "I think if I were as large as you, I'd enjoy shaking myself like that."

"You'd be hurt if you were large like me. Besides, swinging a sword is not as easy as it looks when you've arms this large." He wrapped one around her and picked her up. "It does have its advantages when getting to hold a pretty girl."

He sat her down when Pavel and Trianam came toward them. They both looked spitting mad, and she tried to think why what was going on would do this to them all. The closer they got, the angrier she got until she was as angry, as they appeared to be.

She glanced at Zapps and thought of something. "When we're together it makes us angry. Something doesn't want us to be together so we can figure this out." Trianam started to speak and she cut him off by raising her hand. "We're being manipulated. Something wants us to fight, so it makes us mad at each other until we go our separate ways. Why? Is it the king, or whatever, that I've heard about or something else?"

"Mayhap it doesn't want us to talk to each other, to plan." She nodded at Pavel and he continued. "I've a powerful need to tear your throat out. I've not a reason as to why, but it seems like a good idea to me. And when I was with Trianam just a moment ago, I'd had the urge to run him through. 'Tis not a feeling that I enjoy. Nor, you should know, it's one that I will act upon."

"Aye, I've had the same feelings." Trianam looked at Zapps. "But you've no such desires, do you? You are still as happy as you've been forever. Right now, that sickens me. Why?"

Aurora had a feeling he was right. But the reason that Zapps wasn't affected still eluded her, because he was still with his cousin most of the time. Something was off more than just not getting together. "You've been staying away from us. You and your cousin, you've been gone most of the day and return only at night. You've understood this since the start, haven't you? But you think there is more, don't you? I mean, more than just not getting close to us?"

"I've no desire to harm you and yours. And yes, we have been staying to ourselves, just talking about what we've missed with being apart. I had no idea that he'd been born and he was telling me of my mother. I've not another reason as to why but it seemed..." Aurora nodded. There was no reason that she could see that he was apart from them only in that he did indeed want to talk to his cousin. She moved back to the encampment to think and to try and work this out without killing each other. "It seems to me that it might be what you have been eating. We have, when we are away, make do with what we can find. There is very little of it, but a few branches will fill us for a time."

"You think it's the air or the soil?" She didn't know, and told him that when he approached her with a cup of water. Word traveled fast when there were just the few of them.

"I can't stand the way we fight. Even being alone, all I find I want to do is find one of ye and cut you down," he said.

Aurora was taking a sip when she looked at what was in the cup. Looking up at Vildar she watched him carefully. He'd never brought her a cup of anything before, because he preferred to stay alone as he'd said. Pitching herself forward she spilled the tea. "I'm so sorry. I got a pain in my foot and I dumped it."

He nodded and sat down. While he didn't appear to be upset, she still watched him. Perhaps it wasn't anything more than him wanting to be with them all. To fight? Maybe. But she couldn't see anything from him that would have her worrying.

Then she looked down at the snow. "Where did you get the water?"

He looked at her oddly and pointed to the barrel that hung on the side of his wagon. She walked over to it and smelled it before turning to him. Nothing. Just water was in it, and there was no odor coming from it either. She still had a feeling that there was something off about it. "Where did the water come from? Is it what you brought with you from the castle?"

"Nay, my lady, that ran out a few days ago. I've put snow in the barrel and we've been drinking it. Keeps it mightily cold, which I've enjoyed, but there was no reason for us to go with a powerful thirst so I've been keeping it filled. Do you have a problem with the way I am working around things, my lady?"

She looked around shaking her head. It would explain a great deal. Their tempers were sharper today, even Pavel was short too. And the more snow that replaced the waters that they'd brought in the barrel, the shorter their tempers were. Their need to murder higher.

"I want you to dump this." He started to protest and she cut him off. "There is a reason, I swear. I think it's what is making us so mad all the time. We drink it and cook with it so we've been really taking a lot of it in us. Boil what you use for us to drink, and also to cook. Don't even bathe in it unless I tell you." I have to think this through but I think that the water is what's making us angry." He nodded, and Aurora went to find the others. She was going to make sure they tried to get through this without killing each other. Aurora barely made it to Pavel and Zapps before they drew swords.

This was a nightmare.

Drawing her own sword to stand between them, she told them what she'd figured out.

By nightfall, they were feeling better. And the next morning, she could see a marked difference in their tempers. There were a few flares of it, but nothing like the last few days had been.

When she went back to find the little blades of grass, they were covered in snow as if they'd never been. That surprised and frightened her just a little. There hadn't been any snow falling from the skies since they'd been here.

Getting down on her knees, she dug the snow up, taking care to not get it on her skin. The grass popped up just as soon as she saw the moist dirt. "I need to know when this started. Do you have a clue?" The little grass shivered. "And I'd very much like your name. The king will reward you for your bravery."

"I do have some knowledge, my lady. And I am Jelli, you are the lady of the dawn. You are the one that comes to free us, the champion?" Aurora nodded. "I had hoped so when I spied you the morn before. Whatever you need, I will help you find it."

She asked Jelli several questions. The little blade of grass didn't know when the great freeze had started, as they'd all called it, but it had been a very long time ago. More seasons than they had been able to count. But she did have a good guess.

"Several seasons I think. Mayhap five or more. The last time there was enough sun to warm the ground I was but a seedling. Smaller than the flakes that fell." Jelli bent her head backwards and looked up. "To feel the sun on me all the time would be most wondrous. And to be above the grounds to show off my pretty seeds when I'm tall enough."

"Thank you, my friend." Aurora put her hands around the grass and blew across it. The little blade and those surrounding it laughed as they seemed to thicken and grow. "I want you to stay safe. My men and I are trying our best to get this resolved. Until then, spread the word if anyone knows anything to let you know. I'll be back tomorrow. That will have to be the only way you can talk to me, all right?"

Jelli moved back beneath the earth.

Aurora knew that she should get up and get moving again but she had to think. And thinking right now required that she stay away from the others.

Five years or more. It had been at least five whole years since a tree had budded or even a field of grass was able to sway in the wind. But she thought perhaps with as cold as it was, it had been a good deal longer. Decades longer.

Aurora tried to imagine what it would be like to be cold for so long. The past weeks had shown her she'd never make it in a colder state but this was where she was now and she had to make it work. Standing up, she began walking away from the encampment and toward what she thought was a stand of dead trees. She knew the moment that she was close enough to feel them, that they weren't dead but hiding, as the grass had been doing.

Putting her hand on the first one she encountered, she was happy to know that it lived yet. She was weak, but she still survived. Aurora reached for the next tree, when a sharp wind blew over her. Turning with her sword out, she braced herself for whatever was there.

A man...if that was what he could be called, stood staring at her with dark coal-like eyes. His large body, made of the snow, was disproportioned in places. His hands were huge scoop-like shovels, rather than fingers. She held the blade with tight hands, and watched him carefully. And when he took a thundering step toward her, she told him to stop.

"My name is Maevi. I'm the king of winter and all that you see. I've taken this land as my own and I rule it. I have not given you permission to be here, so explain yerself and I may yet let you live." She watched him bow low and wondered if he would crumble under the weight of it. "But... I have a thought, I've changed my mind. You are most welcome here so long as you don't try to undo what I've done. It's my right as King of the Winter, to do what I feel necessary for my season. You won't interfere, lady of the blade. Or I will kill you dead."

"When you kill someone, they're dead. You are referring to the continuous winter, I'm guessing." At his nod she felt her anger build. "Do you know that the King of Enneahedral sent me here to free up this place? Make sure that the lands are cared for and that the animals and other creatures are safe? How do you propose that I do this when you've put such a strangle hold here? How is this place to be the gardens, if you don't allow things to grow? And how is it that you have made yourself king? The lord of this world has never said a word to me about you."

"I care not for the absent king. Nor what you think to do for him. I'm King of the Winter. I'm here and I've spoken." Aurora started to laugh at his arrogance but just caught herself before she did. "You will abide by my rules? Live here in peace? Not work against me?" the king demanded.

"No, I won't work with you on destroying what the king has deemed wrong. I will do what the king had assigned me with." Maevi nodded once and turned. As he lumbered away, she hoped that it was finished, that he'd just let her do her job. That was a foolish way to think, and she was pretty sure she was going to regret this. "Maevi? You do know that I'm going to destroy you if you don't let up on this hold you have on the earth here, don't you? I'm going to make sure that the seasons go back to the way they should be and you'll be dead."

Maevi turned fully and before she could figure out what he was going to do, he simply disappeared. All that was left of him was a tumble of snowballs that had no real shape any longer. But before she could resume her talk with the trees, he was suddenly there and lifting her off the ground. She'd never even felt him move when he did it. He'd formed so close to her she couldn't get away.

"You don't threaten the king." He slammed her twice against the tree behind her before he spoke again. Aurora could feel her ribs bruise, her breath taken from her as he pulled her to his face. She might have been terrified but for the lack of thought of any kind right now other than her fear and pain. Up close, the man was terrifying with his sharp razor like teeth and his eyes looking dark and lifeless.

Aurora waited for him to say more. To smash her against the trees again and kill her. But he seemed to stiffen, if snow could do that, and then she was dropped to the ground. As she gasped for breath, she looked into the furious face of Trianam as he stood with his sword drawn and his body ready to do battle.

The snow king was gone, not even snowballs were left behind this time. He was simply dust, snow dust.

~~~

Trianam paced back and forth. The snow beneath his feet had disappeared and the dirt, now mud, covered his boot from heel to laces. Every time he looked at the champion, Trianam wanted to run the snow monster through again. His anger was out of control and there was nothing left to take it out on. He glared at Aurora again.

"If you're going to continue to yell at me, could you at least help me move closer to the fire? I'm chilled to the bone." Trianam went to her side immediately and lifted her gently into his arms. "I can walk. Put me down before...I don't think I've hurt this badly in a long time. I might just upchuck on you, Trianam."

"Nay, you won't. Champions don't...what did you call it?" Upchuck? She told him. "Ah yes, you don't upchuck on those that would help you. I'm sorry that I didn't think that you'd be cold after being nearly crushed to death by a man made of snow. Next time I have to kill a snowman, as you have called him, I'll remember to take care that you are safe and warm first."

He sat her down, feeling badly about how she'd been hurt. While he'd been…he had been arguing with Pavel again when he'd heard the trees. Trianam continued to pace after she was settled but he was quieter about it. He no longer yelled at her like a fisher's wife.

"Don't be snarky. You know I was only kidding you. I do thank you very much for saving me. Now, we will calmly talk about what I just told you about. What do you suppose he poisoned the snow with?" Trianam told her he didn't know as yet but he was working on it. "I'm thinking it would have to be something magical. I mean, he was able to take shape from snow and knock me around while he was at it. Where do you suppose he goes when he's turned to dust? Because I'm not sure what you think, but I'm betting that he is around somewhere."

"I have never been as afraid as when I saw him standing there, bigger than my house and as wide too. I had not yet seen you. It wasn't until I cut him, did I realize that he'd had you. My blade, the new one, it hummed with the need to cut him down." He shivered but not from the cold this time. "What sort of magic would it take, my lady, to make such a being? And is it something that we can battle?"

"You crack me up, you know that?" He looked at her trying to remember what she'd said cracking her up had meant. "You're a little freaked out by a self-proclaimed snow king, and yet you have unicorns and dragons galore, and yet that doesn't faze you." He had to work though some of the things she'd said before he could answer her. But she took pity on him and explained. "You don't care that dragons and other creatures run about but a snow king makes you shiver?"

"He is most unusual, don't you think? And the fact that he could touch you, pick you up makes me think that it's more than mere snow that holds him together, as you have said." Aurora laughed and he felt some of his tension he'd been feeling go away. "Dragons have been around since before I have. The king and queen flew the sky like they were a part of it. I suppose in a way, they were. As for the other creatures, I think of you as one as well," Trianam said.

"Whatever does that mean?" He heard the pain in her voice and wanted to tell her he was mistaken. "Do you think I'm like the snow monster?"

"Nay, my lady." He stood up to pace. "You are an oddity to me. The words that you use are foreign, to me as if you speak another language. Your mode of dress, pants of a man, and vest, as that of Zapps. I find this to be hard to understand. Yet, you fight like one of us. You do what we do, you never...I'm trying to tell you that while odd to me, you are a kindred spirit as well."

"Thank you. I think." She rolled to her side and sat up slowly. He tried to help her but she told him she was good. That was another thing he found he didn't understand. She was manly in ways that made him want to be a better man. Yet she was also as tender-hearted as any woman. Yes, she was most odd.

"Have you talked to the king about this? The real one? He would be most upset to know there was a thing saying that he is ruler. Even over this dead land." She told him she had not. "Mayhap, he has run into this before."

"I've not been able to contact him or Miss Beth. It's like...I don't know, it's too cold or something...to talk to them. But I doubt that anyone has run into this before. I'm pretty sure you would have known about it and the king would have mentioned it. But even if he did, all he'd have to do is turn into a fire breathing dragon and melt him..." She looked up at him. "Melt it away."

"Aye, you said that. Melt him away. I believe that would work, but would he not form elsewhere? It's what I would do." She was smiling at him now and he had the most uneasy feeling she was humoring him. She did that well, treated him as one did a child but she never humiliated him in front of others. Just the two of them. A small and unlearned child. "You have an idea. I'm not sure that I'm going to like it but you have one all the same," Trianam said.

"I do. What do you know about boiling water?" He had a feeling she meant more than simply making it hot. Shaking his head she smiled bigger. "When we boil the water, as we've been doing before drinking it, we take out most of the impurities. I'm not sure...we've been better since we've been doing it. Less snapping and biting, don't you think? We've even sat here together, you and me, and had a whole conversation without drawing our blades. What if that's the way we defeat him? That we melt the snow and try to take him out of the picture."

Trianam looked out over the expansive fields. "'Tis a great deal of snow here. What would we use as a pot? It would take a powerfully big one to melt all this. Not to mention a goodly sized fire and more wood than we have here to use."

"We have Vildar, and his irons to put together something to cook it in. Maybe he could help us in that area. As for wood, we can trim out a few of the trees that have been frozen to death. I hate to do it, but it will clear the way for more of them when we're finished." Trianam was beginning to see that this might work. If nothing else, it might melt enough that they could see the grasses and help the trees that did live. "I'll have to check with the trees before we could begin. I don't know if the fumes from the poisoned water will harm them. Not to mention, we'd have to think of what to do with the water when we're done with it. There will be a great deal of that, and I've yet to see any kind of water, have you?"

"Fumes?" She told him the smell, he hadn't a clue what the smell of boiling water could do to trees but, she did. As he put another log in the fire ring where they sat, he thought of what she'd said about the water. "The water, as you have said, we must think of...shall we cool it to dump on the ground and hope that we don't harm what is beneath it? Will we only dump it upon the grass to let it melt away the rest of the...? No, that would not work. It will leave behind the poison that is there, will it not? Or did you have yet another plan?"

Her plans were always well thought out and flawless. She told him more often than not, she was flying by her pants. Trianam never really understood what she meant by that and after numerous times of her explaining it to him, he finally just nodded and moved on. If she had a plan, then he would do whatever she needed to make it work.

"I don't know yet. Not without talking to the trees. Do you know if there is a waterway here like there has been everywhere else?" He told her that the water that flowed through the king's lair also moved by here. "Since the king had never mentioned water issues in his neck of the woods being bad, I can only assume it's okay there," Aurora said.

"Neck of the woods?" Daily he felt as if he needed a scribe with him to keep up with her new terms. "I should think that he has no woods in his neck. He could be hurt by them and then there is the added thing to how he would be a man when he needed. I think that—"

Her laughter made him smile, and he watched her struggle with it before trying again to get her to drink some brew. Trianam knew that she was afraid that she'd get something she didn't want but he would tell her what was in it if she were to take it. He'd been schooled well on the brews that he had now from Genese. And his lady wife had told him a few more. Aurora would not take them, he knew, easily.

"This will ease your pains. And to help you rest for a bit. I would think, even for someone like you, a nice rest will do wonders to help the bruising you took." She eyed the cup carefully, not reaching for it. "I have made you a promise on my blood that I would not give you anything that I didn't tell you about first. You can trust me when I say, it's a light brew only meant to make you rest a little. It might not even put you to sleep."

"I'll drink some only because I hurt so badly." He nodded and put the kettle over the flames again after she took the cup from him. "Trianam, if you let me sleep more than one day, I shall hunt you down and murder you in your bed."

"Aye, my lady." He put the second helping of herbs back in the bag instead of into the second cup he was making for her. There was no point in getting murdered over this. He had a son he wished to see grow. Handing her the second cup he stood nearby to watch her drink it. Uerthe came to her when she was asleep and curled her into his body. She would be safe while she rested.

Trianam went to find Zapps and Pavel. He needed to talk about the waterway.

CHAPTER 2

Illuminaria wandered through the warmed earth until she found what she was looking for. She could not pick it up, but she could look onto its beauty until she could bring Aurora to it when she arrived in the area of the mountain. The flower, always bright and blooming, turned to look at her when she sat down beside it.

"My lady." She bowed low then straightened again. "I've done as you asked, my lady. He is doing so much better than before. The past several days he'd been pacing a great deal in his large lair, but he doesn't seem so remorseful these days."

Philadona, or her sire, had been planted by Illuminaria when she and Envir had first moved into this world. For all these decades, the family of flowers had been helping her. Watching over the keep and now, all this time later, keeping her mate safe from harm.

"He is no longer distressed?" Philadona shook her pretty pedals and told her he was most happy. And he was working harder each day to make this mountain livable for those that were there with him. "That is what he needs. When the champion comes to him, he won't be pleased when he hears that I've been helping her, too. I think him...I fear for him to go mad."

"He might yet," Philadona said. Illuminaria looked at the large mountain in the distance as Philadona continued. "The king has been working of late, he no longer sleeps in the mountain, but in a smallish cottage he has made for himself. I've been told that it has but a single window he has filled with flowers and plants he had picked, and is growing now. The men and women in the villages are more often than not having conversations with him, or just having him for tea and cakes. The villages are prosperous again as well. Happiness moves through the peoples as if it were a water flowing gently down a stream."

Illuminaria wanted him to be happy. More than she wanted anything. But she had a fear, a profound one, that once he heard she was lingering around, he'd be most upset again. Her heart was so heavy that she changed the subject as she tore her eyes from the home of her love.

"The champion is in the gardens. I haven't been there as yet. The world there won't allow me to come through." The flower nodded. "Do you know why I've been barred from my own creation?"

"Rumor has it that there is a being that has set himself as king. They say he has destroyed what was once a beautiful and wonderful world." This was nothing new to Illuminaria. Since Aurora had been moving through the panels and opening them, she'd noticed that a great many people wished to be in charge, yet no one wanted to take charge. She could not wait for her beloved to reign over all the worlds again. "He's harmed the ground in a way that nothing grows. It's said that he's made completely of snow."

"Made of snow? I don't understand. There's no creature made of snow here. I have personally met each person living here. There was no one made of snow." The flower only stared up at her. "If this is true, as you have said, then I think it would take great magic to create one such as that. And to harden the grounds so that nothing grows is something that we would never condone. He is going to have to pay for what he's done."

"Aye, my lady. A great deal of magic indeed. Enough to keep the queen from entering where he is." She looked sharply at the flower. Philadona only nodded her head and looked away. "The trees haven't bloomed there for some time. The grass doesn't cover the ground, and the water no longer flows so that the fish might live. There's nothing there, save snow and awaiting trees. The animals have all died, the fishes left when they could and the plants, ones such as me hide beneath the ground hoping someday that things will be normal again. For all that we have here, the grounds there have no hope of recovering on their own so long as he is there. I do hope that the lady champion can help them all."

"Do you know how she can help them? What she can do to make it alive again?" Philadona didn't answer and that frightened Illuminaria more than if she'd told her no she could not. "We have to do something to help. What is it she needs to make the gardens the way they once were?"

"I know not what we can do. You can't pass over and the flowers are safe where they are. If they should sprout now, or even raise their heads, they will die." Illuminaria felt her heavy heart pound. "Mayhap she will figure it out on her own. She is most smart when it comes to figuring these quests out. It's said when she comes here, a great feast will be given in her honor. That all the worlds will come together to pay homage to the king and his champions. It will be a great day for everyone, my lady."

She hoped it would be as well, but Illuminaria thought this king, and the dead earth was a little more than a simple castle with crumbling walls, or man bent on destroying all the animals because he could. This was magic. While Aurora had a great deal of it, thanks to Ox and Envir, she was far from taking on the kind of magic that would keep the queen away.

"Tell me when you've heard anything. I should like to...can you summon me? Philadona said she could. "Then summon me when you have news. I care not if it's good or bad, but I need to know."

She started to rise to leave and Philadona spoke before she could fade out. She was able to stay longer but still couldn't stand to be visible all day. It was most taxing on her.

"Do you suppose, my lady, that Lady Elizabeth can go to her? Or should the champion be able to go to her?" Illuminaria hadn't thought of that. "I wonder if the king can speak to her as well. They have spoken a great deal, but I've not heard a peep from either of them in some time. Could it be why he paces so? He can't speak to her any more than you can."

Illuminaria looked at the mountain again. She couldn't go to him yet. The mountain area, much like the garden, was holding her back. It was easy for her to look upon where he lived but she couldn't go to him directly. And she was somewhat a little nervous about talking to him anyway. He was...he always would be her one and true love, and she was dead to him. But if he couldn't contact the champion, then he would worry a great deal.

"I shall go to her now." The flower nodded and bowed again. "Should you hear anything else, you know what to do?"

"I do my lady. I do." Illuminaria knew that if she walked to see Miss Beth, she could talk to her for a little longer but if she willed herself there, she'd have less time than it would take for her to tell her everything she wanted. As she made her way to the little cottage, she planned everything she wanted to say. There was simply too much. Draining herself for however long it would take her to heal again would be too long. So she decided to fade out and walk. It would be quicker and she would be able to see her friend for a little longer perhaps.

~~~

Envir was getting worried. He wasn't angry any longer, he'd already gone through that stage of his worry but he was going to blister her when he talked to her again. However, he had a feeling that she wasn't blocking him out so much as something was keeping him from her. And her from him. When he spied Miss Beth coming toward him, he knew she was having the same issue.

"Can you not reach her?" Miss Beth stared at him when he appeared before her. "I have been trying for days. Nothing. If you tell me you've spoken to her, I shan't know whether to hug you or have you yell at her for me."

"I can't reach her." He sat down on his favorite stump and tried to think what they should do. "She is in the garden, is she not? There is something there...something has happened and she can't reach out to us."

"Yes. She left the castle several weeks ago. I had a thought when I couldn't reach her that she was too busy learning what's gone wrong there. But since then I've not been able to breach the walls at all. And I have tried daily, nay, hourly, to contact her." He wondered if that meant she was dead and didn't want to dwell on that. "I worry for her and her men."

"I do as well. I was having a cup of brew with my daughter-in-law when she asked me if I was taking anything to the champion. It had been days, I realized, when she asked. Not the few hours I had first thought. When I tried to reach out to her, it was as if there was a shield up. A force that was keeping us apart. I'm most worried." As she sat down across from him, he could see the worry on her face. "I should like to talk to her, only to see if she is well. I bake when I'm worried and I've a great many things to give to her and the merry men when I can talk to them, I'm afraid. She will eat it and the men will be most happy for the sweets as well. But...if only I could speak to her then I would feel much better."

"I would like to speak to her as well. I've no baking to do, but I've been asked by the men of the village to bring them no more wood. I fear I've taken my feelings out on that pile." He got up to pace when she spied his work. It was a great many trees that had given their life for his worry. "I've talked with the forest. They're searching for her as well. I think that...I hope that there is simply a larger problem than she has uncovered as yet and she's working. But with you not reaching her either...I should like to have her yell at me right now. I know that it's a silly thing to want, but it's much better than to be here and unable to touch her mind."

Miss Beth laughed, and he sat down again. He reached for Aurora again and hit the same wall. A wall of what, he had no idea but it was there all the same. Even going to the building that he'd set up for her there was nothing new. He'd hoped that when she couldn't contact him, or him her she'd get a message to him that way. He wondered, not for the first time, if she knew that she could send him things through the treasure box and not just him to her. As soon as he spoke to her, he was going to make sure she knew that.

"I've been working with some of the stories for them to be scribed," Miss Beth said. He nodded, distracted for a moment, and welcoming it like he'd never thought he would. "I had a memory of a man that lived in the garden, I can't remember his name, but he was most serious about having a place, a kingdom of his own. He came to you, long ago and told you of his plans to be a great leader and to have a spot of land of his own. I don't think he was thinking of the whole area at the time but I wonder... Do you suppose, with the closing of the walls, he's been able to make himself ruler?"

"Of what? The trees? Mayhap the flowers make his meals and clean his earth for a little of the attention he might bestow on them?" He looked at her stricken. "I'm so sorry, my lady. My temper has been short these days. I fear for her. Please forgive me. But I don't remember such a man. That doesn't mean the conversation is not there, just that I can't remember it."

"I have been as well. It's why I've come to see you." She stood up and drew her sword. Envir had a moment of panic, not knowing what she'd do when she handed it to him pummel first. "Should you like to play, my king? Practice a bit with the blade to get our minds from what is worrying us. Mayhap something will come to us when we aren't worrying about our champion, but where we might be stuck if we make the wrong move."

He took the blade and smiled at the weight of it in his hand. Standing, he marveled that one as small as Miss Beth could carry such a heavy weight. Before he could ask her what she wanted in her play, he felt a shimmer of something evil touch them.

Shoving her behind him, he brandished the blade. There was nothing he could see, but he knew that something was close. When Miss Beth moved to stand beside him, he noticed that she too had a blade and hers was at the ready. He didn't expect to see Aurora fade into his glen.

"I don't have much time," Aurora said. He nodded, a thousand questions popped into his head but he didn't voice them. "A being is keeping me from doing my job. He is using magic that I don't know how to beat. Nothing you have given me...nothing have works. My soldiers may die with me here if we can't figure this out. You must come to me at once and see what you can do for me. I need you to come now."

"What do you need from us?" Miss Beth moved forward. "You are hurt. Did he do this?"

"I have something for you." She looked to her left and he could see the faint outline of something, but it was too blurry for him to make out. There was white and nothing more but too large by half for a cloud. "I need for you to see if you can figure out what is in it," Aurora said.

Then as suddenly as she appeared, she was gone. He called her name twice, reached for her with their connection again and again but felt nothing more than he'd found there before. It was as if a window had been closed between them and had only opened long enough for her to ask for some help.

He started to tell Miss Beth he could not see a thing when a flower appeared where he'd been sitting. Envir dropped to his knees to see if the little plant could use his help. Miss Beth put her hand to the back of his shirt and held him away from it. He looked up at her when she shook her head.

Almost as soon as he leaned back from the plant, it listed to the dirt and died. The plant, one of his, simply died. He looked at his friend to ask her what had happened.

The fire shot out of her hand like she'd been holding a torch. He leapt back from her and the flame as she set it to the dead plant. Before he could ask her what she was about, the flower flared up in a great black smoke, much too large for the size it was and then disappeared. Envir looked at her.

"It wasn't her," Miss Beth said. "Think about what she has said to us. All the times that she spoke to us, did she ever say those things? She never called it her job, it was her quest. They aren't her solders, but her merry men. Whoever that was, it wasn't our Aurora. I would bet my life on it. And that thing there...I've not an idea what it was, but it wasn't from her either. She would not...I don't think she knows that she has the ability to bring that to you."

He looked down at the now blackened plant and wondered why it was here. Envir suspected had he touched it as he'd been about to do, he might have been ill. Or killed. Whatever had sent it, meant for him to be harmed. He stood up and moved back from his former champion. As soon as he did, he set a flame, this one hotter than anything she might have produced, into the earth as deep then more as the roots might have been.

When he was satisfied that there was nothing left to taint the ground, Envir shifted back and moved away from the area, towing Miss Beth with him. He wished to put as much distance from where they were and the thing that had come to them as possible.

"Do you think it knows, whatever it was, that we killed his offering? That whatever it had planned for us failed?" Miss Beth shook her head then shrugged. He had a feeling that she was correct, they would not know. "Whatever it was, the thing pretended to be my Aurora, do you believe he has harmed her? Killed her?"

"Nay. I don't. She has a part of our blood, yours through her drinking it and mine because I'm of her blood by family. If she were dead, I believe we'd know it." He had thought the same thing and was glad that she'd said it too. It reassured him in ways that he had not thought that he'd need. "With this thing coming to us, showing us what he can do, we can now figure out how to help her do you not think so? We have more than we did before. Something wants us to not be able to help her I think."

Nodding, Envir thought of all he'd told them with his visit. "She is hurt. Wherever she is, he has harmed her. I think so because he would only be able to appear as her as the last time he has touched her. It would be freshest in his memory. There is magic that would do that, take the image of a being and be able to reproduce it in a manner that you'd think it was them. But it would be only what they saw. They could not change when the person did. Do you understand what I am saying?"

"I do. And that is true. We have…remember long ago, that man that I was talking about? The one that wanted to be king?" Envir nodded. "He had a bit of magic. Not a great deal but a little. You told him that should he improve on them, make them more useful to the kingdom, then you would present him with a spot of land he could rule over. His own land, not that he was sharing with his neighbor."

"I only meant to appease him by giving him a house and a bit of dirt that he could plant a garden in, not make him a king." She smiled at him and he glared. "Will things forever come back to haunt me I wonder? Will I need to keep my mouth closed when people come to speak to me about things that are better left to the drawing board whither they have come?" Envir asked.

"I would think so. I doubt that it's in you to do, but I would like to see it. As I would guess many would." He wanted to tell her to go away but that would do neither of them any good.

"Maevi. His name, it's Maevi." She laughed and Envir decided that he didn't much care for Miss Beth at the moment. "You did that on purpose. Distracted me so that my mind would no longer be trying to remember him. I really don't care for you right at the moment."

"I did. And to a good end, as well. I remember him now, Maevi of the gardens. But surely he is dead. It has been centuries...nay, more than that since we have heard from him." Envir didn't want to point out that a great deal of that time, he'd been resting while things around him had not but he could see in her expression, she had thought of that as well. "Do you suppose he improved? And now he has it in his head that he is now the ruler of whatever might be there?"

"It would seem so." He sat down again and tried to think. "He said that he...she said that she was going to die. Do you think he was telling us that she wasn't going to beat him? That he thought perhaps killing me, because

I've no doubt that was his plan, will keep her from saving that world?"

"I would think that you are the key or the lock as it may be, to whatever is going on there. Even if he only thinks that you are dead, he will act according, you think?" He looked at Miss Beth, trying to figure out what she meant. "He came to you. The flower was for you. I think had you touched it, or even smelled it you'd be dead. For some reason, he believes that with you gone, she won't be able to defeat him. He must know of the connection between the two of you. And knowing that, he would know that without you, she will give up. I doubt that she would give up with you again, but beings that have large heads rarely think things through well."

"I have something, some thing or some knowledge that will help her, you are saying?" Miss Beth nodded. "What could it be? And once we have figured it out, how do we get it to her?" Envir said.

"I don't know, my lord." She stood and he watched her as she lay out a number of things on the ground. He'd not even noticed that she'd brought a pack with her until that very moment. He would need to keep better track of himself and his surroundings. "I have these things to give her. I know not how to get them to her or what she would do with them, but I feel the need to get them to her," Miss Beth said.

The items, a half dozen or so, were a mismatched bunch of things that one would find in the yard and around the home, or better yet, in the trash bin. There was a lantern that had no wick, a blade that had not seen a whetstone in a while, and a length of leather bound together with some string. He picked up the kettle that was dented and dark with age. The small pouch labeled *head powders* he left where it was, as he did the pair of work boots, also worn with a hole in the toe. With the kettle he picked up the large stone and held it to the sun. It was an opal. The milky stone had a large blue vein running through it. None of it made any sense to him or apparently Miss Beth.

As she sat there she began to move things around. Matching he supposed, to each other to see a pattern as to why these particular things. All he could imagine was that she'd gone through her rubbish bin and this was what she'd found. Envir wanted to kick the lot of it away and try to think how to help her.

But the moment he turned his head, something caught his eye. Bending down he picked up the lantern and pulled the glass shield from it and set it upon the ground. Then he picked up the opal again and laid it in the center of it so that it was seemingly trapped within. It was right. He had no idea why, but this was the way it was supposed to be.

"If the sun hits that, it will become a flame. The opal has the blue vein which is what I use to light my stove." He nodded at Miss Beth as she spoke and thought about the being. Envir refused to think of it as Aurora, his Aurora, as he moved the other items around. Sitting back on his knees, he looked at Miss Beth.

"Snow." She looked at him not understanding. "Behind the being, there was snow. A great deal of it as a matter of fact. At first I thought it to be a cloud, white and fluffy. But it wasn't. There should't be snow in the gardens this time of year. It should be filled with greenery, the trees in full bloom," Envir said.

"He was standing in it. Deeply too, it went to his knees. I never...you're right, it's the season of blooming there. There were no blooms, no color at all. I didn't even spy a blade of grass and we were seeing her...him fully." He nodded. "That's what is wrong, the weather is wrong," Miss Beth said.

"Yes, but why?" She didn't know and said so. Neither did he. But he had a feeling that was going to be her quest. He played with the items more, moving one to the other but leaving the opal and glass bowl from the lantern where it was. That, he knew for some reason was working. The rest...it went together but how, he wasn't sure.

"There are other things I had a notion to bring her. Not things like this, odds and ends that I had to find." He turned to her and she smiled. "Aye, this stuff wasn't just lying about my home. Some was in the barn, so dusty that I was ashamed with my cleaning. Even had to get my good son to come help me get to some of them. These things were what I wanted...nay, what I needed, to make sure she had."

"He must have thought you off a bit, your son." She smiled and laughed. Envir looked around the fields where they were. "I've not an idea what she will think when she gets here. There is so much...it seems perfect to me. What trials must she be going through to do as I need her to do? To unlock a land that I thought to be resting as I had. I can't tell you how, daily I feel as if I've failed all of you."

"You failed no one. You brought her to us when we were without hope. She woke you when we needed you most. She is doing everything we need to be one world again. And without any training. I've grown quite fond of our champion." Envir nodded, he had as well. "You don't think she will lose do you, sire? You think she can beat this thing, do you not? To be honest with you, I will be most upset with her if she should fail now. Less than half to go and I find myself getting more and more excited as she comes to us," Miss Beth said.

"I do. She is brave and strong. Stubborn to a fault. There are times when I wonder should I murder her or hug her first." He laughed. "I actually fear doing either to her. She might want to run me though with her blade should I try."

Miss Beth laughed, too. "I would do neither, until you are assured she is unarmed, my lord. She can be quite scary when she is in battle mode. Even her men, they'd run you through for her, I think. They are loyal to her like none other I've ever seen."

"I miss her." He moved a few more of the objects around to try and buy himself time as his heart ached so. He'd talked with the young champion every day for months now and he was missing her terribly. Her wit, her smile. And yes, even her sarcasm and biting ways about her. He wished he could do something to bridge this gap between them. And even though it wasn't of either of their doing, it was something that hurt him deeply.

After a while, Miss Beth went home. She told him she was going to work on some of the items, since she had her list. Envir thanked her, but knew that it would be him to figure it out. As Miss Beth had said, he was the key to this.

One of the farmers he'd been working with came by just as he was realizing it was lunch time. Elvar picked up the leather and before he could tell him to please leave it be he looked at the old kettle. Then, picking up one of the boots, he pulled the lace free. Wrapping the length around the handle then the lace, he grinned at Envir. It was as if a light had gone off when he sat it over the glass and opal.

"'Tis a good pot holder. And it doesn't flame up easily, as it has been tanned well. My misuses, she has me saving my old leather all the time, so that she is able to wrap her handles." Envir nodded knowing without a doubt he was correct. "I've come to see if you would like to have some sup with us. We're having an outdoor cook as we're preparing for some storage of meat. The neighbors are coming, too. Everyone is bringing something to hang and cure. Good of you to allow us to do this, sire. 'Twill make it a sight better when the cold comes and the animals are deep in their holes."

Envir told him he'd be there. As the man walked away, he turned back when Envir called his name. "Elvar, why did you assume that the leather was for the kettle? I mean of all these things, why those objects?"

"You've the bowl and opal there. A good one, too. 'Twill flare to life, a good sized fire. The other things too are for a fire as well." He asked him how. "The blade will cut the sticks that you'll need to get the flame started, the leather goes hold the glass should you wish to move it off once you have it to flame. You've a good start for some cold nights or a fast meal should you wish one." He looked at his assortment of things and noticed that one still wasn't accounted for.

"And the head powders? What would one use those for?" Elvar laughed. "I mean except for the headaches I mean."

The farmer came back and picked up some of the dried grasses that had been becoming more prevalent as the days grew shorter. He piled them in a neat stack, then he set the glass bowl atop them. The opal, he placed gently in the glass and almost immediately, a fire started. Its flames hotter than Envir had been prepared for. Elvar used a little of the left over leather and pulled the bowl and opal off and blew gently on the small flames, until it was a nice fire. Picking up the bag of powders, he tossed a small pinch upon the fire and Envir jumped back when a cloud of dark blue smoke billowed up from the flames. The small explosion not all that frightening but startling all the same. Both he and Elvar laughed as the flames turned to a rich blue and heated the area close to them quickly.

"My kids, they love it when we do that. 'Tis little, I know but they enjoy it." Envir nodded, his mind going a mile a minute on what sort of applications that this could be used for. And any that would help Aurora. "Sire? Are you unwell?"

"I'm fine. Fine." He looked up at the man who towered over him. He seemed to realize he was as well and dropped to his knees. "Don't do that. We're friends. I'm your king, yes but we have become friends of late."

"We have. But I've no desire to stand above you. You are my king and my friend but I won't disrespect you in any way. Come to think on it, I would not like to be you. Nor should I like to be in your boots. A man like you...well, I'm glad you're king and not I." Elvar smiled shyly. "I'm privileged you think of me as your friend. As I think of you, sire."

"It's Envir, when we're alone." Elvar nodded, but Envir had a feeling he'd continue to call him king or sire. He sighed heavily and leaned back on his hands to regard the man in front of him. "The champion is in trouble. These things here...they are a link to her somehow. There is a being there, one that plays at being her and tried to harm me. He thinks he will defeat the champion and do...I've no idea what he has planned for me but he has tried to harm me and mine."

"Harm you?" Elvar sounded so indigent that Envir had to laugh. "Shall we gather our forces? I know a good many men that...Sire? I think you should explain. I've no way to go to her aide if we've no idea how to get there. I think once again, I am glad not to be the king and only the friend to one."

He did. In great detail explained to him what had happened since Miss Beth came to him, up until Elvar came to tell him about the leather and other items. And not just the events of the day, but everything. He took him to the shed he'd made to send her things. Showed him how she came to see him, if only as a specter. Envir told him of the tales he'd heard, the way she'd come to be with him, and he also told him his fears for her. The man nodded. Asked questions, good ones when necessary and listened to him. When he had spun the tale the best he could, he sat down again on his stump, exhausted.

"She is a true champion, then. You hear of things when you are sitting around working but you've never a mind to know what is truth or not." Envir nodded at Elvar. "I should like to give this some thought. May I share your tale with the missus? She has a sharp mind, she does. Mayhap she can think of something that we have not."

"I would like that. But please tell her to keep it to herself as well. I don't want everyone to know of Aurora's tales. It may yet upset others to know that she has so little in the way of training." Elvar nodded solemnly. "You're a good man, Elvar. When we are all together again, the champion and I, I should like to hire you to work for me. I need a good man. Mayhap my champion could use you as well."

"You honor me with your praise, my lord." Elvar walked away and Envir saw that his step was a little higher and his head tilted up more. The man had become a good friend and he was going to make sure that anyone and everyone knew it. Envir had only a few hours before he met them for the last meal, and he found himself looking forward to it more now as well.

CHAPTER 3

Aurora woke to the sound of cursing. She never really understood the words they used. They were not really curse words like she'd heard in her world, but more of a low garbled of grunts and growls. She rolled to her side, winced a little then sat up. She had to blink several times before what she was seeing really made much sense to her.

"What are you doing?" Both men, Markard and Vildar looked at her. "You're making enough noise to—" She'd started to say, *to wake the dead,* but once before when she said that, she'd had to explain that it'd been a joke. She had to be careful what she said to these people. They were a very superstitious group and at times took things quite literally.

"He dropped it, my lady. Shifted it in a way that it hurt my hand and I had nary a choice but to drop it on the ground." Vildar glared at Markard, who was looking like he was ready to pull his blade and kill the man. "And my finger? 'Twill never be the same."

"Let me see." He came forward, and even before he got to her, she could see it was more than likely broken. It was bent at an odd angle and his nail was darkening. The swelling was already bad, and the bruising was turning it a nice shade of purple. Instead of coddling him, she laid her hand over his injury and looked him in the face. "It needs to be splinted, but first we have to straighten it out. Do you know what I'm saying?"

"Aye, you're going to hurt me." She smiled and nodded. "I'm a good man, my lady, but I fear that I won't be singing your praises when you do it. I've a feeling that you might wish I was gone from you rather than hear what I might be calling you."

"I understand." She looked at Markard. "Can you get me some binding and two flat sticks? They don't need to be very long, just about the length of his fingers and we'll work from there. We'll have to bind it with them so it will heal well."

Markard took off and she looked at Vildar again. "I don't want to hurt you. If you'd rather wait on one of the men, I'm sure they'd be able to do it. But the longer we wait, the more the swelling is going to be, and that much more painful."

"They would but I doubt they'd be as nice about it after as I'm sure you will be, my lady." He nodded to his finger. "While we're alone, do it. I've also no desire to hear them tell me I've come to be a baby about it either."

She jerked the finger back into alignment. He sat down hard but he neither hit her, nor screamed. She would bet that he was cursing up as storm in his head but he never said any to her. Aurora told him to breathe slowly in through his nose and out his mouth, until he could see past the pain. He did as she told him, and by the time Markard came back, the swelling had gone down and Vildar wasn't nearly as pale.

After seeing to his finger, she stood up. She noticed that Markard was staring at the large pot she supposed they'd been working with when the accident had happened. It looked like he could have stewed a large boar in it. Markard smiled at her when she asked what it was.

"I asked him the same. He said it's a melting pot." She nodded and wondered what on earth he could be melting that he'd have to have something this large. Unless it was one of them. She asked the two men.

"Nay, 'tis a way to melt the snow. We just have to figure out a way to heat it." She had thought of this, too, but where to put the water. The trees, she had to talk to the trees.

"I'm going to go to the small glen where we were yesterday. I was wondering if one of you could go with me, so I can talk and not be beaten to mush while I do it." Both men nodded, and she smiled. "You both don't have to go but thank you."

"I'll go as well, my lady." Uerthe moved toward her. "You are better today? You took a hard beating yester-eve. I worry for you when you let someone hurt you thusly."

"Sore but yes, better. And so you know, I didn't let him hurt me so much as he took it upon himself to knock me around. I had no idea that snow could move that fast." Aurora knew that he'd held her through the night. And she thought that somehow he'd healed her by doing so. She'd never asked him if he could do so, and really didn't want to know right now. Instead, she moved to sit upon his great back and he took off toward the sky.

The wind was warmer up here. She could see that the area was as white as she feared it would be. There wasn't a speck of green anywhere. Even the trees were bare of anything more than just branches covered in the snow, that seemed to just appear over night without a drop of it falling from the sky. When Uerthe moved his great wings up and down she could see the snow move about the ground and wondered if she had them all do that, would the plants have enough sun. Even for a little while. He answered her unspoken question. She'd forgotten about their connection.

"Nay, my lady. It will only make them more starved for what they can't have. We will get them sun soon. I have faith in you." She was glad someone did. "We all do. You should as well. Look how far you have gotten us."

"I know." But she felt like she'd failed them on this one. What was she supposed to do against a monster that could move faster than she could see and had everything here thinking him to be king? It was disheartening to know that she had no idea how to beat the monster. "Do you suppose that someday, I'll be able to just take a nap? You know, just lie down and not have a care in the world for say...two months?"

He laughed, it rumbled her seat and she giggled with him. "My lady, the day you willingly taking a nap, I shall lay down beside you and we'll rest together. But I don't see that happening, even when you get to the king. You don't strike me as a woman of leisure. I would think it's not in your blood. This thing that we are set to do here, it will make us stronger, I think." If it didn't kill them while they were at it, she thought.

The king. She'd been trying to reach him since they'd gotten here. And at first, she'd thought he was blocking her. But she was sure now that the creature was doing it. Aurora shivered when she remembered his cold breath on her face, the way he'd tossed her around like she was no more than a twig. When Uerthe started his descent, she watched as the snow came up to meet them, the way that it scattered about, leaving a bare spot in the dirt for them to land.

The trees were there, but they were covered in snow. Their tops and branches so heavy that she feared they would break. As she walked up to them and touched them, she could feel their cold, it seeped deeply into their wood and she gave the one she touched just enough warmth to wake it.

"My lady." The branches shivered off their heavy burden and she sighed. "I've been so cold for so long, I thought never to be warm again. Your touch brings me both happiness and sadness. What is it I may help you with today, my lady champion?"

"I know, and I'm sorry for that." Aurora gave the tree just a little more, and begged her help. "I've been trying to figure out how to rid you of this weather. I think that once the snow is gone, all of you will be able to wake. Is that true?"

"It is, my lady but there is a problem. Once the snow is melted, the waterways will be tainted as well. Once the sun, her majesty in the sky, tried to heat the soil beneath but so many of my sisters died from the poison, she was forced to stop, hiding herself away from this area but only to light up the day and not heat it as she wishes. She has been hiding this past years, so that she won't harm any more of us." Aurora looked up into the sky. "She is a great person, the sun, but she can't help us until the snow is gone," the tree said.

"When the snow melted off, do you know where it went?" The tree shivered again and Aurora had a feeling it was going to be bad. "There is a waterway, isn't there? And it's frozen."

"From mud to top." Aurora tried to think how, if the water was frozen, did it move beyond this point. The lady of the tree must have known what she was thinking because she answered her question. "There is a stream, well below any of us can reach well. Our roots have gone deep, taking away some of our strength to get to the water. It moves to the outer lakes and streams, the fish have gone that way we have been told. It's well and good for them to do so. There is no reason for everything to die if it can get to a safer place. Do you not think so?"

She told her that she believed that as well. But she thought of what she was saying. Tap roots, Aurora thought. The trees had adapted by making a tap root. But if the waterway was frozen solid, then she'd have to figure out a way to heat it enough to thaw. That alone would take more heat than she knew how to produce.

When she left the glen, the tree asked her to take back her warmth. She told Aurora that it would be easier for her to rest without it. To be chilled for so long, the warmth, she claimed would make her sad when she started to freeze up again, and she didn't want to be thusly so. As she pulled the warmth from her, Aurora also caught a few of her memories.

Lovely ones of when they were bursting with flowers and fruit. There was a great many of them gone now, more than she had thought possible. Saddened by the truth of what had been done here, she turned to see that the monster sat in the snow. He was glaring at Uerthe, who had his body tensed for attack. She wasn't sure if the creature thought to harm him or was waiting on her to return to finish what he'd started yesterday. Either way, she was ready for him.

"Why have you done this? What earthly reason could you have to make it so cold all the time?" He looked at her and smiled. The sharpness of his teeth, large ice shards made her think of the bully on a childhood favorite Christmas show. "You've nearly killed everything here. Not just the plants and trees, but there is no game here, nothing for anyone to survive on. Tell me why you would do such a thing. I can't believe that you've done this for meanness."

"I did. As I am going to take your lives from you for doing what I've forbidden you to do. I told you not to interfere with what I've done. Beside, what's to survive here? As you have said, I've made sure that they are all dead. The plants have no use now that there is no human's or creatures to eat them. So the game was as well, and I made sure that there was nothing here to disturb my peace. As you are doing." It occurred to her then that she'd not seen a single person since she'd gotten here and wondered if they were in hiding, as they had been when they were being hunted by the candel. "I see your mind working. Are you worried about your king? He is dead you know. I killed him meself just yesterday," the monster said, laughing.

"You lie." He laughed and she reached for Envir again. There was nothing there, a void but she knew as surely as she was talking that he wasn't dead. "How did you pull off this grand feat if you killed him? No one can reach him. You have cut all communication off."

"That I have, that I have. But I have the power. And I don't lie about this." He stood but kept his distance from Uerthe. "And you will die as well, champion. I will kill you and your soldiers and that will be the end of this job you have been set on."

"So you know who I am." He shook his head and told her that he knew what she thought she was to him. "I am the champion. And you will know I'm going to make sure your plans were for not. I'll bring this area back to its former glory with or without your help. Then we'll see how you like it when you are no longer king of this place. Because I got news for you buster, you are going to regret messing with my world."

"You think so," he said. She nodded and drew her sword when he took a step toward her. "I'll not harm you. Not yet at any rate. I wish only to touch you."

"I don't think so." Aurora had a sudden thought about what he'd done to her yesterday. He could've easily done more damage to her than he had. But he'd only wanted to touch her then. To...to see the king. "You visited the king as me, you took my image and you made him think that you were me. You went there and pretended to be me and that's how you think you killed him? He's much too smart for such a childish trick. And now here you are, needing to know why whatever you did didn't work. Because you know, don't you? That it didn't go as you'd planned. I'm still here and...And I'm going to defeat you. You have to know that."

"He should be dead. I killed him with my magic. He is dead." Aurora told him she didn't think he was that powerful and that he'd failed. His voice roared over her and she smiled. "He should be dead, not planning and trying to cut through my magic to defeat me. He won't, I tell you. I'm ruler here. I don't want him here. He has promised me a spot in the kingdom and I've claimed it. When he shut the gates around us, it was my duty as the lord of this area to lay claim before anyone else did. He wished it to be so."

"I doubt very much he wished you anything but ill will. You're a mean and nasty minded being that is going to go down. What has it gotten you, to be king? Who are you ruling here? You are the king of nothing. Less than nothing. There is no one here for you to rule. Nothing for you to make grow. And you have killed every living thing here so you are alone. And will be forever. You are the king of frozen water." He growled low but didn't advance when she laughed. Then it occurred to her that if he went to the king, perhaps she could as well. "If you did indeed talk to the king, show me. Let me see how you've done it."

"I won't be tricked." She shrugged and moved toward Uerthe. "You have not been dismissed. I demand that you stay and talk to me," the monster said.

She turned then and stared at him. He was lonely, just as she'd said to him. The man who'd set himself up to be king was lonely now that he had all he wanted. Aurora moved again toward her wings and got upon his back. As soon as she was settled, she told Uerthe to move. They were skyward before the frozen king could touch them.

"He wants our company now, I think. At least until he kills us as he has claimed he would. What a strange creature he is." Aurora told him she thought so. "He will seek you out now I think. He will come to you and try to get you to talk to him. He misses the art of conversation. The feel of someone face to face with him. Why would he do such a thing if he knew that he'd be alone, my lady?" Uerthe said.

"I have no idea. But I won't talk to him until he gives me something in return. I wish to see the king, the real one. And I need to get him a message when I do." Uerthe told her it was a good plan. It'll be if I can figure out how to talk to the real king without having this one trying to kill me again. We'll also need to be careful that we don't let ourselves be trapped by him. I have a feeling that he'd take one of us just so they would have to listen to his voice."

She was on the ground when she realized that she'd not seen Trianam for a time. When she asked Tholan and Zapps, they said that he'd taken Eritai, and had taken to the skies as well. She was looking up when she saw him, a small pinpoint high above.

Aurora was sitting near the fire when Trianam came to her. As he sat down, she could tell by the look on his face that something was bothering him. As the men drifted away, Aurora thought he'd speak then, but he only sat there, his face tight with whatever he had on his mind. She spoke of what'd happened with the snow monster today. And what she might have figured out, concerning the man.

"He said that he is king of all things." Aurora wondered if he meant here or the entire world but, figured that he mean everything. Which was nothing really at all. "He said that the dragon king told him he could have a place to rule. I'm not sure I know what to think of that. I can't see him doing that, can you?"

Trianam told her not to think at all, it mattered little what she thought or did. Aurora felt her temper rise. To have him, of all people tell her to give up made her think he'd gone mad. But before she could say anything else, he sliced his fingers over his throat, a trick she'd showed him, and she snapped her mouth closed.

He looked around and then leaned closer to her. She found herself leaning in as well and was surprised when he spoke so loudly. Trianam winked at her when she stared to pull away.

"There is something about here that afears me, my lady. I've been worrying about it for hours now." She frowned at him. "I don't think we can defeat this thing. He is very powerful. And very strong. Smart too, if you want to know the truth. Much smarter than you or I."

Before she could speak, he put a sheet of paper in front of her. There was writing on it, and she was stunned with what was there. She wanted to ask him how he knew but he only pointed to it.

"He watches and listens," the paper read. She looked up at Trianam and nodded. "I guess we should simply wait then until he kills us all in our sleep. I don't know for what, but we'll wait. Maybe he'll forget about us and we can live out what is left of our lives here. The cold will kill us soon enough."

He nodded and leaned back. "What say you about the monster? Do you think him to be a better king than the dragon? He is not here so…"

She wanted to bark at him to shut up, but stilled when she thought of something. Aurora wondered on it for a few minutes as Trianam continued talking as if she were a part of it. If he had to pull down the magic, if only for a bit, she could send the king a message though the box. He'd sent her things through it, and she could more than likely send him something back. She started writing on the pad of paper as she spoke to Trianam. Once she was finished, she handed it to him, then started on the note to the king.

He laid it back down and she glanced up at him. Trianam nodded and she felt like this could work. If she could get the monster to open a pathway to the king, she'd have Trianam put a note in her treasure box. Hopefully it would go through and she'd have a way of getting the king information. If nothing else, he'd be able to see what he could do on his end to send them blankets and stuff to keep warm.

~~~

Illuminaria waited for Miss Beth to come home. She supposed she could've waited in the house, but she didn't feel good about that. When she spied her coming along the path, talking to herself, she moved toward her. The closer she got, the more nervous she felt. It wasn't until Miss Beth looked up, did she seem to notice her.

"I'm sorry to come to you like this, but I can't reach Aurora. And I can't go to her to speak to her either. It's as if she had a dome over her that I can't breach." She nodded and moved into her home. Illuminaria followed Miss Beth into the house and noticed her surroundings. "What has happened here? Have you been set upon by thieves? Oh my dear friend, what have you lost? I will find a way to get it back to you this moment."

The kitchen was a shambles, so unlike the fae's usual neat room, that she worried what might have been taken from her. Boxes of flour and mashed corn were overturned, there was a broken mug lying about on the floor, its handle under the rocker that sat close to the fire. The hearth was full of ash and some of it had blown over the table and the dirty dishes there. Even her rubbish bin had been overturned. The trash from it, strewn all about the floor and table as well. Miss Beth only sat down and burst into tears.

"I'm sorry, my dear." She wished she could hold her but there was nothing for it. As she cried, Illuminaria moved about the room, looking for some clue as to who had broken into her home. When she blew her nose, Illuminaria turned to her.

"I've not been set upon. This is how I left it. I know it's hard to believe, but I was looking for things I thought that I could take to Aurora. She is in need of my help and I can't go to her, either." She stood up and began to clean the clutter, a rag was brought from the sink and the ash moved to the hearth once again as Miss Beth continued. "I had a vision while breaking my fast. I saw these things...I know about Aurora. I tried several times to go to her as well and I've gotten nowhere. Then I had this...this whatever and I had to take some things to the king. It was seemingly useless things but I'm sure he can figure out what they are about."

In short order, she had things set to right. Illuminaria had listened to her and made a note of the things she'd taken to Envir. As Miss Beth wiped down the table, she sat down and smiled. "I'm sorry about before. It's been a strange morn. Then when the creature I was telling you about showed up, it was just too much on my heart and I just had to cry about it. It's hard to be brave all of the time and I found I could no longer hold it back."

"I've been so worried, when I couldn't go to her or speak with her. She is in the gardens. I so loved it there." She had, too. Walking through the tall trees, the flower gardens with their neat rows of pretty little heads above the greenery. "What has happened that we can't reach her? You believe it to be that monster, the one that tried to harm you and my love?"

"Yes. And magic. Very strong magic that can even hold the king out. You too now know what we know. She can't, we assume, reach us either. Then that thing came...I hope she is well." Miss Beth told her again about the visit from the monster. "He came here to kill the king. I believe, as does the king, that his lordship is the key to getting to her. I don't know what to do. It burdens my heart terribly that I can't get to her. Frightens me as well, if you want to know the truth of it."

"The monster, you think you know his name?" She told her it was Maevi. Illuminaria searched through her memories for the man, and came up with it. "I remember him. He was a great hulking man who would shout every word he spoke no matter the setting. He had it in his head about something too. I know not what it was, only that it was something we would not have entertained at all. Something about ruling for the king so that he could rest. Envir rarely rested when he needed to, and said as much to the man. Then when he left, my Envir had told me that he said the man could have a plot of land, should he learn to improve the area that he was living in. It was just a house we thought, not an entire world."

"That's him." Miss Beth set a flame to the hearth and put her kettle on as she continued. "He came to you both once again to ask about being a ruler of his land. He was told that his magic, though it wasn't strong enough to support being ruler, would have to be made into something worthy of a ruler. The king told us later, after you had...you were one then that he said as much to him, so Maevi would work harder. I do believe when the walls came down, he took it upon himself to rule there. The snow covers everything.

"Not the trees. I mean, it might cover them but they would still live. Had they not, would we have heard about it? Nay, not the trees. The flowers of the earth would have told me if that were true." Illuminaria thought for a moment. "Perhaps you can get her a message through them. I know that the plants would be gone, but the trees have no such luck. Mayhap if you sent something to her, a message that you are worried, she would get it."

"That's it." Miss Beth danced around the room, spilling her tea as she went. "I could tell her we are worried and we want to know is she is all right. And if she has any information to relay it back to us. We could communicate that way to finish this through them. I had not a thought to try that, my grief so profound in not being able to go to her and help."

"I think it's worth a try." They made a list of things to tell Aurora. She knew that the trees would give her the message, but if it was too long, it could only get messed up or miscommunicated. As she finished up, Illuminaria followed Miss Beth to the trees. The first one of many messages until they were able to go to Aurora was being told to the big elm standing near Miss Beth's garden.

Miss Beth turned to her and smiled. "The champion awoke one of the trees long enough to speak to her. She is well, as are the few men with her. The girl is trying to figure out a way to talk to the king. She wants him to know she is well. She also said that the monster has spoken to the champion, and the meeting didn't go well."

"I would think not. And that is the best news." Miss Beth nodded and smiled as she leaned against the tree. Aurora would get the message, but it would take a while for her to get it. Sometimes trees could be very detailed about things and take forever in the explaining. Especially when they were excited and in a hurry. When she pulled away from the tree, it bowed to them both before standing tall and straight again.

"She is making a deal with the snow monster the tree told me. He, as I've said, came to the king and she is going to have him prove that he can talk to him. When he does, she is going to have Trianam put some things into her treasure box and see if they will get to him. I have said we will send what we have as well. Along with what we think they are for." Miss Beth was hurrying to her home. "I must get some cookies going and some bread. They must be near starved for something warm to eat."

Illuminaria watched her go. Her time was at an end and she was fading fast. Calling for Miss Beth she waited for her to turn before she used the last of her energy to make herself whole. "Have him send her the *Book of Fae*. She will need it soon."

Miss Beth nodded as Illuminaria felt herself fade away. She was getting stronger each time Aurora finished a task, but it still drained her so much when she was solid for so long. Letting the darkness swallow her up, she thought of the girl that was going to save her Envir. He'd be so happy when she got to him. And mayhap, if Illuminaria was lucky, she'd be able to see them both together before she was gone, for she had no doubt that when the champion finished her quest, she would be finished as well.

Illuminaria knew what was happening was only because she was needed by Aurora. Her magic was somehow tangled with hers, and the two of them were as one for a time. Somehow, Aurora's magic was helping her to be aground for just a little longer. It both saddened and made her heart fill with joy at this time, a time when she would have missed it all when she'd been murdered.

CHAPTER 4

Aurora had the tree repeat what she needed to do twice. It was unfair of her she knew but to be told to have all her men at the treasure box was unreal. What were they going to bring out? Trying not to think about what might or might not happen she gathered what information she could on the area, including what she could see from the sky and about the taproot, and put it all down.

She'd been a pretty good artist when she'd been home. Drawing out designs as they came to her made her get size and proportions correct too. So drawing a picture of the great monster wasn't hard, but getting any kind of perception with the lay of the land without much in the way of landmarks wasn't easy.

"What should I say? Go to this pile of snow until you get to this one? Won't work." She turned to look at Tholan when he laughed. "I talk to myself all the time. I'm not nuts."

"I would say that is a fair assessment of yourself." He sat down. The big troll no longer made her feel as if he was going to squash her, but she didn't feel as comfortable with him as she did with his cousin, Zapps. "I wonder if you could answer me a question, my lady. It's about the trees," Tholan said.

"If you want to know how they can talk to me, I have no idea." He shook his head. "I'll answer you as best I can. I'm still learning as I go along too."

"You are doing a good job. None other could have done what you have done and come so far as you." She flushed at his compliment. "Nay, I was wondering if they have told you where the water is?" the troll asked.

"It's deep down." Tholan shook his head and smiled. "Then I don't know what you want to know. I guess I should really shut up and let you tell me, shouldn't I?"

"It's also not in your nature to shut up, as you put it. You are a thinker and thinkers, such as yourself need to speak. Nay, I was wondering if they told you that they gather around it. The water is just inside of them. If I were to go above the skies, I would say it looks as if they guard it. Like they are a circle around them for some reason. At least that is how it appears to me as I walk around them."

"Guard it? From the monster?" He shrugged and his muscles seemed to take on a life of their own. For such a soft spoken man, he was huge, his one arm would be as big as her waist, she thought. "You think that they gather around it to protect it? If not from the monster, then what? The snow perhaps? No, that doesn't seem right, does it?" Aurora mused.

"I know not. But I've spent many a day here before the great closing. And I know where the lake lies. As for their protection, I don't know for sure, but they are gathered about it." She wanted to call to Uerthe and check it out. But Pavel came to them just then and she asked him if he wouldn't mind checking out Tholan's theory. He nearly leapt at the chance.

"They have been feeling very un-useful of late. I would say if you asked them to sweep the snow in a long path for the day, they would fight to be able to do it themselves. They are bored I believe." She knew the feeling. All this sitting around and waiting was driving her a little over the edge, too. At least they were no longer snapping at each other. "Might I make a suggestion?"

"Yes, anything." She thought he'd tell her that she should set up an exercise program. But she doubted very much any of them would do jumping jacks and if they did, they'd grumble the entire time. But when he stood up and helped her stand as well, she waited for him to take her somewhere.

"There is a thing we trolls play at. I'm not sure if the humans, or even Pavel have a similar game but it's a good one." He took one of the logs, a small one that looked smaller in his hands than she knew it to be and put it on the ground. As he kicked it to her, gently she noticed he told her to kick it back. "You are to try and keep me from making a point. We shall make the wagons, they are far enough apart for us to play, and we shall call it home. I will take this one, you the other."

"Soccer." He looked at her oddly. "It's a game we played where I come from. The children love it, and some adults are pretty good at it too. But we used a ball." He said they would use a large round stone. "We'll have to keep an eye out for one then. But for now, the log will work fine. So long as we're careful not to stab ourselves with it or to get a splinter."

She kicked the log, really too big for her around for a few minutes. It wasn't long before both Trianam and Markard had joined them. Soon they had a good game going, with her and Markard on one team and Tholan and

Trianam on the other. Zapps said he would track the points when he arrived about five minutes into the game. They were laughing and having a great time and she knew it had been a long while since any of them had had this much fun.

Pavel returned shortly after her team lost to Tholan's and they all sat down. Trianam was still arguing about the size difference being an unfair advantage, but he was very good-natured about it. She thanked Tholan for the suggestion of the game. Aurora could already see that it'd made a difference.

"I've seen what Tholan means. The trees are in a circle, but around what, I can't tell," Pavel announced. She asked him how big of an area did he think it was. "I would say about as big as ten wagons end to end going both ways. It's a fair amount of area. If there is a lake there they protect, then it's well beyond any that I've ever set my eyes to."

A large lake. She was thinking how long it must have been for it to freeze solid. A lake that big would have taken decades. Aurora knew that time had little to no meaning to these people. She enjoyed that about them. But sometimes, like now, she was a little frustrated about it. Taking a deep breath, she let it out slowly and looked up when someone said her name.

"My lady, I have an idea that you are being summoned," Zapps said. She looked in the direction the troll was pointing. There stood the monster, and he was looking at her as if he had a great secret. She wondered if he knew about their plan. It frightened her just a little, that he could hear everything that they said.

"It's the lack of buffers. Trees and grass would make sound less loud for us." Trianam had told her when they were in the air just this morning, he could hear a great deal more than had they been in the pasture or any of the other places they'd been. "As you were talking just before I came to you, I was a good fifty or so footsteps away. I could hear you as well as if I was standing next to you. I believe he can see us to for the same reasons. We must take care as to what we are saying. Any mention of the king will have to be made in other ways."

After that, she'd had the men put the wagons far apart and whenever they needed to speak, it was to be within the wall of one of the two. Aurora had no idea if it would work or not, but Trianam had told her the wagon filled with trees was the most difficult to hear from. He claimed he had to come nearly atop them before he could understand a word. That was where she had been sitting when Trianam told her she was being called for.

"Can I help you?" Aurora asked the monster.

Maevi looked around as if he didn't know who she was talking to. "*You*, may I help you with something, Maevi? I don't wish to be out and away from my men very long. Say whatever it is you think I need to hear and let me get back to where I was. There is at least a fire burning there."

"I have thought it over." His voice roared over them and she put her hand on Zapps when he took a step forward. "It's good that you keep your animals in line. I should hate to have to kill them as well. Not that I care if they or you live but for now, I wish to prove something to you."

"Really? Well, I don't care what you think to prove to me. You wish me harm and I don't like you. Whatever you have to say, I've decided that I don't care to hear it. And don't call him an animal again. He's not an animal, he's my friend. You'd do well to remember that. Now. Say it and be gone. We've not bothered you and I expect the same from you." He growled at her and she raised her chin. "Acting like a baby will get you nothing but ran through. You know that we can do it. We've done it before," Aurora said.

"You were lucky in your blade. You won't be so again. And I will prove to you that I've killed the king." She stared at him and wondered how she was going to make this happen without all her men there. Then she saw Trianam coming to her from behind the great monster. "You'll see that I've killed him and you'll bow to me," Maevi said.

"I don't think so." He took a step toward her and stopped suddenly. She knew that whatever had stopped him had a great deal to do with Trianam. When Maevi turned, she could see that her man had his sword laying against the monsters frozen body.

"You cut me, and I will kill you. It takes too much for me to make myself whole and I've no desire to have to make myself again and again." She tried her best not to be excited about the information he'd just given them. "I want to talk to the girl. She and I have business."

"You have business with her when she says you do. Not before. And I don't take my orders from you, monster. She is my champion and I only listen to her word." Maevi turned to her as Trianam continued. "She will say nay or yes. The champion has the final say in all that we do. You don't, no matter how much you claim to be what we all know that you are not."

"Champion? He thinks you to be her, the champion? She is not you." Aurora quirked a brow at Maevi. "I have met her, you aren't the champion but a pretender.

Elizabeth is the champion, you are nothing more than an imposter, no matter what spills from your mouth."

"No. Miss Beth, Lady Elizabeth, retired. I'm the new champion. And if you're here about killing the king, I've given it a great deal of thought and there is no way that you've—"

His roar this time sent shards of ice toward them. Putting up her hand and powering some of her magic out, the ice stopped just short of hitting any of them. When he only stared at her, Aurora took a step toward him and was glad to see him take two back. The tip of Trianam's sword sliced through him and she could see the ice forming on the blade. He didn't move and she thought perhaps he was afraid to. Perhaps he would need to be sliced, not just stabbed.

"You will learn to curb your temper, or I swear to you I will show you the meaning of getting medieval on your bad self." He nodded once and she could see a little more fear in his ice blue eyes. "As I was saying, I don't believe that you've killed the king, the dragon king. Had you done so, all of Enneahedral would no longer exist." She had no idea what would happen if Envir died or got hurt but the monster in front of her didn't know it either apparently. "Now, I've no more time for your foolish games. Go back to wherever it is you came from and leave me to my—"

"I will show you." She shook her head hoping she wasn't making a mistake in playing this the hard way. But she was afraid that if she jumped at the chance, he'd turn her down for spite. "I will take you to the place where he lay dead. I will show you. Then you will know that I'm a man of my word some of the time."

"Some of the time? And how? How will you show me something that can't happen? You think to hurt me? To kill me with this so called magic of yours?" He smiled at her and it was scary to say the least. "I'm not going anywhere with you. Especially nowhere where my men can't see me."

"I will take you now." He put out his icy hand and she only stared at it. She needed time. Not much but enough to let the king know. Looking at Trianam he pulled his sword from the monster's body and stepped around him. She looked at him, hoping for just one thing to go right. His smile told her that he had an idea and she was willing to jump right on it.

"I would suggest, my lady, that you take a moment to think about this," he whispered to her, but it was loud enough for everyone to hear, including the monster. "The last time you hastily did something, several people died and there was so much blood. Mayhap you should take a moment." Trianam winked.

She started to ask him what he was talking about but he winked at her. It was so out of character for him, she could only stare at him. Then he put his finger under her chin and closed her mouth. That got her going. Yes. She needed a moment to tell the trees, then the king.

"A moment then?" Aurora asked.

He nodded once at her request and she started for the grove of trees. She knew that someone followed her and knew without a doubt it wasn't Trianam. He would guard the monster. When she was at the line of trees, she turned and looked at Markard and Vildar.

"My lady? Did you really lose your temper and kill men?" She shook her head at Vildar and he nearly sagged with relief. "I knew not what he meant, but I thought if you had done such a thing, it would have been for a good reason. You are a good champion with a hard heart when it calls for you to have one." While she wasn't sure how to take that, she was on a mission and would deal with him later. The things that came out of that man's mouth made her think he was a little weird sometimes.

Aurora leaned to him, close enough to whisper in his ear. "Remember. He hears us. I must speak to the trees. Watch."

He nodded and stepped back. When he leaned to Vildar and told him to watch over her, he nodded as well. Turning her back to the two men, she touched the tree she'd spoken to before.

"It's time." The tree swayed gently. "Tell him my men will stand by. Tell him...tell him that I'm sorry."

"For what my lady? He will ask, no doubt." She smiled. No, he would scream and shout, but he would not simply ask. "Our king is a most wonderful man."

"He is. Tell him I'm sorry for not being able to do this without bothering him." The lady of the tree swayed again and Aurora held her hand up, warming the bark until she felt the tree's happiness.

"The king said to tell you to buck up and to stop being whiny." The laughter coming from the tree made Aurora smile. "He also said to tell you he is looking forward to a sword fight with you, to kick your bottom. I'm not sure that would be such a good idea, my lady. I have heard of his ability to fight and it's something that stories have been written about."

Aurora laughed as well. "Tell him I look forward to it and he shouldn't be so cocky." She warmed the tree just a little more. "I'm sorry to have to wake you like this. I know that it's cold for you. I promise you, I'm doing all I can to help you all."

"We are honored to serve you, lady champion. My sisters and I have been helping more. We have searched our roots out and the moving water is now saying it will do as you ask. He will call to the fishes as soon as you tell him it's safe."

Thanking the tree and her sisters, Aurora dug her fingers into the cold frozen ground and sent a little of her magic to the soil. She hoped that soon she'd be able to heal all the grounds, but for now, she wanted to help those who had risked so much to help her. When she came out of the gathering of trees, she looked at her men. Both of them were on duty and ready, she was very proud of them in that moment.

"I'll need you to stand by." Both of them nodded and put their hands over their hearts. She had knighted them both, gave them a part of herself just yesterday and was glad now that she'd taken the time to do so. Reaching out to them she touched the mind of Vildar. Aurora felt his fear, his uncertainty. But she also could feel his honor, something she hadn't expected. Markard was afraid as well, but his fear was of failing her. Or himself. He was the most unsure man she'd ever known. When this was done, she was going to have Trianam work with him a little more. When they stood, she nodded to them both and moved toward the monster. They were as ready as they'd ever be.

~~~

Envir stood just behind the tree. Hiding yes, but a necessity. When they arrived, he was going to be out of sight until the men and women of the village could pack all they had into the shed. Every day he was gladder he'd enhanced that big building with his ability to send things to her. Had he not, then all, he was afraid would be lost.

When he'd gone to dinner last evening with Elvar and his family, he had told them everything that was going on again. This time telling them that not only was Aurora in trouble but that they could help him. He told them what he needed. Elvar's lady wife was indeed as sharp as he'd been told, because she had a long list of things that the snowbound warriors might need. Including things that he might never have thought of. Like wine and cured meats.

After he'd given permission for the rest of the village to know also, within an hour he was flooded with blankets, foodstuff and warm mittens. There were large hanks of meat, cured for the winter, and dried herbs of all kinds. There was a stack of drawings from the children, thanking them for what they did every day and telling them to hurry to them, they wanted to meet all of them. Someone had even put together a cord of wood, dried, split and ready to be burned. Envir was nearly overwhelmed to the point of tears at their generosity. And when he thanked them, each of them, they told him she was their champion as well and what she needed, they'd provide if they could.

And now they stood by, ready to put in as much as they could in whatever time they had. He hadn't felt the magic before, when the creature had arrived. Just an evil feeling that had been so fleeting that he'd been sure he'd missed it. He'd been so focused on speaking to Miss Beth, but this time he felt more of it, all that it was. The darkness of it, the tainted evil of it nearly took his breath away. And as he waited, hoping to hear Aurora's voice, he was as still as he could force himself to be.

"You see. He is gone. Buried no doubt." The voice was cold, he supposed it should be but it was the dark kind of cold that made him think of storms that destroyed, where people, *his people* had been killed. Of men with sharp blades and sticks. Of peoples that would kill rather than turn to understand what it was they were killing "You will bow to me now, charlatan. And I will have no more words of you being the champion."

"Not so fast there, big boy." His champion, that was his Aurora, was speaking now. Envir had to tighten his grip on the bark of the tree he so wanted to go to see her. "You say you killed him and all right you say that. But there would be something here, don't you think? Some kind of marker, to say that this great guy had been murdered by a snowman? I mean, he's *the king*. Someone would've have noticed that he was laying here dead. Why isn't there anything like that? Why? I'd think there'd be at the very least a large rotting body, don't you?"

Her wit. Even now he wanted to demand that she be respectful. To speak...then he realized something that he'd not though of before. Her sarcasm was as much a part of her as his dragon was of him. She dealt with things, things she didn't like with it. He wanted to go to her then and tell her he understood. But the monster spoke again and he stood where he was.

"I tell you, he is dead." Envir looked at the shed some distance away. The men were working frantically at filling it. And he had a feeling that Aurora's merry men were working just has hard. Every time the door closed when it was filled, it would reopen almost immediately. It was working, he knew it was. He had a thought, one he would file away for later but he was going to try something else when this monster was dead and gone from his gardens. The creature had done enough damage.

"Lord Envir?" He heard her shout his name and still he waited. "Hey king, where are you? Is anyone there? Hello? Miss Beth, where are you? Does anyone know where the king is? Is he dead somewhere? I've been told that he's dead and I'm here to—"

"Why do you call her?" Maevi asked.

Aurora said something he missed.

He didn't hear what Aurora said but he smiled when Maevi spoke. "No, I fear no one. Especially a retired champion, as you have said. It matters little to me if you call them all. But my time is running short. We must go. You have your proof that he is dead, do you not? He has not answered your calls. That is what you wanted to know and now you see. I have killed him."

Envir stepped around the tree and stared at them both. Aurora was dressed in so many layers of clothing that he almost didn't recognize her. But he did the man. And when he jerked her back, pulling her in front of him, Envir felt his dragon want to take him. But he needed a cool head if this was going to work. Taking a deep breath, and letting it out slowly, he smiled tightly at them.

"What on earth do you do here, Aurora? Should you not be working on the jobs I've set forth for you?" She grinned at him and he felt his heart leap. This child could take any situation and make him glad to be a part of it. Even with her being held in the arms of a monster such as this, he wanted to laugh with her. "You think I pay you to come and visit me when it suits you? Nay, I don't. Get yourself back to your work. Now, if you please."

"You sure are bossy today, kingie. But I have a question for you. This guy said he killed you. And that's why I'm here. To see for sure." They both looked at Maevi, who was staring at Envir as if he'd seen a ghost. "He said he was the new king, and I had to do his bidding. And we both know I don't do that well. I don't bow to you, much less to someone who lies all the time. It's good to see that you're not dead," Aurora said.

"No, you don't bow to me at all. You are rude and sometimes even disrespectful, but you do work hard." He glanced to his left to see that they were still working at the shed and then back at the two of them. "Why did you think you killed me?"

"You were poisoned. I did it myself," the monster said. Envir took a step toward the man, forgetting that he could not touch him any more than he could Aurora when she entered his space. "You are dead. I know not what magic you are using here, but I'm not fooled by it. I have killed the dragon king and I will be ruler of all that I can see."

"You must not be able to see well then. As you can see, I'm not dead." He sat on his stump as his knees were a bit wobbly. Miss Beth had been right, he had been the target. Envir was afraid to react badly and get them all killed for it. The man had tried to kill him; he'd admitted it for all to hear. "Do you know the penalty for trying to kill the king? I assure you, it's most severe. As you have admitted it, you face death. By her."

"I fear not this woman. She has tried to beat me and has failed. You will as well." Envir looked at Aurora, who was smiling at him. "You think that she has any way of defeating me, she would not have tired it again by now? I am a mightier king than you are. Her puniness has nothing on the power of my magic," the monster continued to rant.

"That's treason. And by the way, I'm pretty sure if you faced her man-to-man, you'd be surprised at just how un-puny she is. She's strong and brave and my champion." Maevi roared, and droplets of water, not ice, touched his face.

He looked at Aurora and reached into her mind. *"He is melting. Good gracious, if he stays here, he will be gone. Do you think we can play with him a bit more and just have him water the grass he is standing over? And come to think of it, how is he here melting? You aren't...you're here? He has brought you here."*

"Of course he's here. What the heck did you think we were...you thought it was the same principle as the blade? I don't know how he's doing it, but what of me? When he dies here, with me, will I die here or go back to my men to do so? His magic holds me, right?" He felt his fear double now, taking the place of his happiness just that quickly. *"I don't know what's going on, but I'm pretty sure if he dies here, so do I. But the fact that he's here, that's something I hadn't thought of until now. He really is here. Not me, I don't think."*

All sorts of things entered Envir's brain. If he was here, which it seemed he was, then Envir could destroy him with just a breath of his dragon. But she was right, what happened to her? Did she die because of how the magic was pulling her here? It wasn't worth the chance of killing him to find out for sure. Then he'd just have to bring the man here without her. But how? Then it occurred to him.

"You say you are a better king, is that correct? You say that you tried to kill me once and of course failed. Is that correct?" Maevi nodded. "Then let's test that. You fight me. We'll have a duel, you and I and we'll see who is the better king. If you were to win, then it would be truly as you say. If I win...well, then things will go back the way that I had them. Without the snow and ice to cover my gardens," Envir said.

"A good idea." Maevi moved his hand through the air and it changed into a long swords. "You will die this day, imposter. I will slice you to ribbons with my magic. Skewer your body so all may see my power."

"Not now," Envir said. Maevi looked so disappointed that he only just caught himself from laughing. "In one hour. I will be waiting you are the large field to your right. That way you can take my champion back and ready yourself. I fear now it would be an unfair fight, with you melting the way that you are. Don't you think?"

"Why do you need for me to take her back?" Why indeed. His mind raced to find a reason. Nothing came to him and Envir was afraid he'd failed her once again. But then the monster spoke up. "You are correct in this, I can see that having her here would be a distraction for me. I will return her because she will be pressed to step in where she is not needed. And that would be unfair to our fight. I shall take her back but not because you have said so but because I wish it."

Envir stood up. "We shall meet in one hour. Until then, you will tell me what you have done to the gardens."

"I will tell you nothing, dead king." And with that, he and his Aurora disappeared. Envir sat down then leapt up again. He rushed to the shed to see the men and women standing there celebrating. They had done it. They had put all that they'd brought and the things he'd had place into the shed. Envir hugged them, each and every one of them. He just hoped that on the other end, things went as well.

"Sire, it was a good time that we had," Elvar said. Envir nodded at Elvar as he was handed a thick rolled parchment, as well as a few things that he could not make out. "A grand time indeed. And since we made it work, we were wondering if tonight we could have celebration of sorts. The good champion will be able to defeat the monster, and we'll be that much closer to having our world complete once again."

"I'm afraid we'll have to wait just a bit longer for that celebration. I have to fight him," Envir said. Elvar staggered back and was only held up by his missus and another man. "In one hour, I have to fight him. But I do so as my dragon. He is a monster, I will be as well. But I would wish that you'd have the field cleared of everyone. I don't want any of the people hurt by either of us. "

"Nay, sire, you are no monster. We have seen you, you are a good and kind man who is our king." Envir nodded, distracted now. He thought of Miss Beth and how angry she was going to be. "Sire? I'm sorry, sire, but I don't believe any of us will leave you to fight him alone. We'll not interfere, as we've seen you both in your larger form, but we'll be there in the event that you might need us."

"Thank you so much, Elvar. You become a better friend daily. I was thinking of Lady Elizabeth, however. She's going to murder me." Envir looked up when he heard his name. "Ah, here she comes now. I will admit to you, Elvar, she scares me a bit more than the snow monster does. A good bit more."

They were still laughing when she reached him. Envir could see the fire in her eyes and wondered how she'd found out so quickly. But before he could ask her how, she started in on his character, his parentage as well as his lack of good sense. It was all Envir could do not to laugh. But he loved this woman and knew that she'd cut him to ribbons if he did.

"Of all the stupid, childish things to do. What do you think he will do to you once he returns? Do you think him to bow before you and say what a mistake he made? He won't." He started to tell her, as a dragon he could defeat a man made of ice but she continued on before he could. Sitting down he waited on her and wondered not for the first time, how he had managed to live so long without noticing what a joy she was.

He glanced down at the papers and wondered if he could read them now or after he fought the dragon. Thinking he might not make it, for stranger things have happened of late, he asked Miss Beth if she would be so kind as to help him with it. She huffed at him and took them from him.

"This doesn't get you from the hook." He corrected her. "I don't care if you are off the hook or not, you are still upon my list. And correcting me is not getting you in any better graces with me, my lord."

"I know. But we are under some time limits for now. Should you like to yell at me later, I will allow you all the time you think you might need. Until then..." He looked at the papers again. "Aurora needs our help. Please?"

CHAPTER 5

Aurora dropped to her knees as soon as they were transported back to the gardens. Her entire body hurt. She dug her fingers into the soil beneath the snow and begged them for forgiveness just before she took from it. The pain in her body started to dissipate almost immediately, her vision which had been blurred became less dizzying and her belly no longer wanted to spill everything from it. Whatever magic he'd used to take them to the king, wasn't something that she'd ever want to do again.

She knew the others were close by. Trianam's boots were in her vision now and she had to smile. He needed new ones, she thought. As did the rest of the men. Markard was arguing with someone but she couldn't tell who. For now, she was content to just sit the way she was and try to feel better.

"We've more supplies than we can handle I think. Never thought they would stop coming." She nodded and leaned back on her heels, looking up at Trianam, who was smiling.

"You look ill, my lady. Mayhap, something didn't agree with your belly," he said.

"I don't know what he did to me, but I thought I was going to die." He nodded but never moved. "Is he around? Because I have to tell you, I'm tempted to find him and kill him myself."

"Nay. He didn't come back with you. Not sure where, he's gone but I didn't see him. Only you." She started to stand but couldn't. "You'd be better served to let me bring you some stew," Trianam said.

"Stew?" He nodded and whistled for one of the men. It was something she'd taught him the other day. "What sort of stuff did he send us? And if you tell me that there's bread to go with this stew, I'll give you everything I have," Aurora said.

"Aye, we have bread a plenty. Some still steams with warmth. Butter too, should you like it. But there is a collection of strange things. And many things that we will need more than ever, should we not get rid of the monster. Blankets, some food stuff. Wood too, enough to keep us going for a long while. Even pulled out half a stag that was cured. Never thought he'd be that generous."

"You make is sound as if he sent us his kingdom. Just how much did he send us?" As he moved out of her sight, she looked just behind him. All she could do was stare. "Did he leave anything for the people there?"

Aurora looked up at Trianam laughed. "I thought the same. I don't know what we're to do with all of it. Burn the wood, and feast on the food. Some of the things, like the stew, is still hot. There be a tin with your name on it. I think it be cookies from Lady Elizabeth." He laughed again when she moaned. "You be the strangest woman when it comes to your sweets. But there is plenty to share, should you have a mind to. She might have cleaned out her pantry with how much there is."

Sitting down on a log they'd been using for chairs, she was handed and large wooden bowl and a spoon. The smell of it nearly had her leaning her head into the bowl and lapping directly from it. A large hunk of bread, still warm, was shoved into her hand. Just as she was taking a large bite to her mouth, Trianam spoke.

"'Tis hot so don't drink it down too quickly. I've no time to see to your burnt tongue. In addition to everything else I've been doing. Vildar nearly burned his off when it came through. Had to bury his poor mouth in the snow." She grinned around her first bite. "Good, is it not? There be plenty, so get your fill," he said.

As she finished off her second bowl of stew and fourth piece of bread, Aurora sat with Trianam. He was having the men make a list of the stuff as well, as sort it into piles. The cloth, and everything that needed to be eaten right away, was stored in one of the wagons with the wood under it. The stag would be cut up and stored deep in the snow to keep it from going bad. Other things, things they had no clue what they'd do with, were put on a list for her.

There was a wind chime that was made of pretty stones. A stack of thank-you notes that she read to them. Also, a sack of things with her name on it. She opened it last, as well as more bags of seeds to plant and even a thick pillow someone had taken the time to embroidery a pair of dragons on. She pulled the sack with her name toward her and laid the pieces out before them.

"What do you suppose this is for?" The glass bowl was beautiful and she was surprised when she was told it was the glass from a lantern. "And this? I doubt the king would want me to make me a necklace right now."

"Nay." Pavel took the beautiful opal from her and put it inside of the glass. "'Tis a fire starter. When there be enough dried sticks beneath it, it will flare up almost immediately. The head powers, they will make a magic show for you. Turn the flame to blue. Mostly kids like it. Makes them smile. You think the king is thinking we've nothing to do but have magic shows?"

Parlor tricks. She never said it but she wondered what he thought they were doing over here if they had time for tricks too. Instead, she looked at the kettle. Then at Vildar. He was grinning at her.

"I suppose you know what to do with this." He nodded and told her he did. "Well? Want to tell us?" Aurora prompted.

"'Tis a way to heat water." She wanted to smack him in the head. "I could fashion a big one or two, perhaps big enough to bathe in and we could pour it upon the lake. Might help with the melting." He showed her in the snow how he could fashion it for her. "I'd make it on wheels so it would be easy to roll around. And a drain here at the back so that as the snow melted out, it would pour along the ground to water what we've uncovered. I could...there is another lantern we can use and I could make it so the heat was constant. Burning a little at a time so that the pot was forever working even as you moved."

"Do it. You say you have enough to make two of them, and have the heat to make them work this way?" He told her he did now. Aurora looked at Trianam and he smiled. "He sent metal workings through?"

"Aye, he did. I wondered about that, but now I can see what he was thinking." Trianam nodded as if he was just coming to realize they might make it out of this. "He sent us things to keep our chins up, my lady, and things we'd need to get by. Our king, he's a good man, he is. I'm proud to be working with him and you."

She had told them about the fight, the duel between Envir and Maevi. Pavel spoke up when she finished the conversation that had been between the monster and the king. "You think the king will win?"

"I think he'd better." As they sorted through the things, she realized she could melt a great deal of the snow at once. There were things here, in the pile of items she didn't have a clue what to use them for, others she could see their function as clear as day. As the men drifted off to help Vildar with his work, Trianam sat down again. This time he looked pleased.

"This came as well. It was wrapped up in a tight bundle and had my name across it. Said I was to make sure you got it alone." She took the large cloth and felt its connection to her almost as soon as she touched it. "I've no idea what it is. Precious is all I could think to know."

Aurora unwrapped it slowly. And as more and more of the book, because she could see now that it was indeed a book, was unveiled she could feel its magic and power. By the time it laid in her lap, its cover showing, she was almost afraid to touch it. But she knew what it was. And had known the moment she'd touched it.

"The Book of Fae," Aurora breathed. As she opened it and thought of the vial of liquid that the queen had given her so long ago. Reaching for her satchel, she pulled the lovely bottle to her. Looking at Trianam she pulled the cork and drank it down. She was both excited and sad when nothing happened.

"Can you read the words?" he asked. She looked down at the cover and saw the words, symbols really, suddenly, they seemed to reshape and move into straight lines of words. The longer she stared at it, the faster the lines moved into a language that she could read. Aurora ran her finger over the heavy script and told him what it said.

"Forever the Book of Fae." She read the second line twice before she told him what it said as well. *"The holder of this book, holds all that we are."*

After opening the thick and beautifully designed leather cover she looked at the first line. Aurora felt her blood run hotly through her veins before she spoke to him again.

"It has my name here. Aurora Kirkpatrick, Last Champion of the Kingdom of Enneahedral, Lady and Knight to all who live." She looked at Trianam. "What do you think that means? I'm going to fail and this is my story?"

"Nay, I think it be your story, but not that you shall no longer live. I think it means you are the last champion. No other will follow in your footsteps. You will reign the champion forever." He looked at the drawings that had appeared as soon as she'd opened the book. "Good image of you. You thinking it waited until it saw you before it was ready to put you there?"

"That would be my guess. How would anyone know what I look like?" She closed the book and ran her fingers over the decorated cover. "Someone took a lot of time with this, don't you think? I mean, just look at the gold and silver here. And the jewels. This alone makes me want to hide it away and keep it safe."

"'T'would be a shame, my lady. I think you are meant to it. Might help you and us in the coming months." She nodded still overwhelmed at the beauty of the thing. "If you come across anything we might need, you let me know. We're going to beat this, to my way of thinking. And when we're done, we'll settle down and make a boring life for ourselves." he said.

Aurora had been thinking a lot about where she'd go after this, how she'd return to her world and what on earth she'd do once she got there. She knew that she'd been told she was to stay here, but what was she to do? Knit? Collect cats like some women did? No. She didn't think she'd be able to stand that any more than she'd be able to live in the other world again. This book, along with Trianam's words, finalized what she'd known all along. She was never going home.

"I had a life there. Not much of one, but I had one. No one…I've often wondered if anyone would know if I died in my apartment. And how long I would rot there before I was found? One person, Annie, she was my friend but not like…not at all like you and the others have become to me." She didn't want to sound morose but it was hard not to when everything she'd ever wanted was suddenly hers for the taking. Only, it was in a place that no one she knew would ever come to see. "I'm to stay here. I won't be able to ever go back, will I? I mean, they've told me before, even you have, but this makes it seem so real now. I'm going to live here all the rest of my days."

"Aye, my lady, you are here to stay. And a better place it will be with you with us. To think, for all of my life I didn't have you there and now I can't imagine a world without you in it." His voice was so soft, so comforting, it was her undoing. Putting her hands to her face, Aurora cried. It wasn't as if she was unhappy, no, she was happy, thrilled beyond words, to know she was going to get to live out her days here. "My lady, I never meant to make you cry."

"It's fine. I promise you." She looked up at him and he smiled at her. "You are my best friend, Trianam. I don't know what I'd do without you, either. You are simply the best friend a girl like me could have."

When she finished acting like a baby, because she did feel foolish afterwards, she looked around. Trianam had left her to go and fix their noonday meal, so she went to find her men. They were playing a game of soccer, and they seemed to be having a grand time. It appeared as if in their bounty, someone had sent them a large ball.

"Someone made it for us." She picked the ball up when it went out of bounds. Markard, flushed with excitement, showed her how they'd made it. "They took a stone, a nice round one, and wrapped it in cloth and other materials. This one is a fine one. Someone took the time to wrap it in tanning. We can have this for years. Others will come and join us in the sport as we move through the worlds. Mayhap the king will play a game with us."

As the sun stated to set over the mountain, she thought of the king. Hopefully he was smart enough to know that just because it looked easy, didn't mean it was. The arrogant man would more than likely get himself killed and leave her all alone as to do a grand job of things. Whoever would she fight with if he was gone from her life?

Just as she was kicking the ball to make a goal, Aurora felt the pain rip over her, taking her breath away, she fell to the ground to try and get it back. The second time something tore at her flesh, she screamed. Glancing down at her body, she could almost see the blood pour from her wounds but knew they weren't hers. Just as she felt another blow to her, she realized that someone was screaming at her, begging her to tell them what had happened. Before the pain, incredible pain, took her away, she forced words out.

"The king. He's hurt."

~~~

Miss Beth watched in horror as the big dragon fell. She had wanted to go to him several times, to draw her sword and end it, but Elvar held her back. It was his fight, the king's fight, he said, and he must be the one to end it.

Maevi, the snow monster, was far from uninjured himself. The fire had raked over his body over and over, and had taken a great toll on him as well. Most of his left arm was gone, his right gone to the shoulder. His legs were burnt as well, their icy limbs no longer strong enough to support him. But 'twas his face she couldn't look upon. Most of his head, from chin to top was melted away and the man, the human man, stared back at them. His own body eaten away, she thought by his madness. She could see the man that had been and how the monster inside of him had taken over.

"I could have won. Should have." Maevi's words were labored, slurred even as he fell to his death. His body lay in the green grass as it melted too. Ribs that were once covered in skin were exposed when the ice was gone, his belly, now open was nothing but an empty bowl made of melting ice. The man who was the monster was dying. And she feared that her king was as well.

"What you should have done was serve the king." She wanted to kick him in the head for his stupidity. But she had to see to her king. When he had fallen, she had to wait until he shifted back to man before she could help. Now she ran to him with her basket of herbs and rags.

"Is he dead?" the king demanded.

She growled at her king and he had the nerve to laugh at her. "You are a wonderful woman when you do that. I think you care for me just a little. But you must please help me so I don't look poorly in front of my friends. I wish to go back to my home."

"You die, and I will let you rot here on this field. I shall embroider you a sign that says *'Here lies the king. He was a fool.'* How could you do this to me?" She wiped at her tears as one of the women from the village helped her tear his clothing away. "You've a burn here that runs deep. I wondered if that was your heart there for but a moment. Then I remembered you had none. I should...you should be...what am I to do with you should you die? You have my heart, you old fool."

The woman sitting next to her gasped. Miss Beth supposed she should curb her temper, but he'd been hurt. Again. When she had the wound packed and wrapped, he was helped onto a gurney, a door from someone's house it looked like, and taken to the closest cottage. Elvar and his missus had cleared their table for him.

"Take me to your house," the king said. She only shook her head at him and told him to hush. "I'll feel better about not taking their table if you were to take me to your house. These people have given me enough. I don't wish to disturb their meals, as well. Do you not think it would be hard for them to have a fine meal with my broken body upon their table?"

"I said, hush. You will hurt their feelings." He looked at Elvar who was helping her cut his pant leg up to the long gash in his thigh. "These people have given you their home because they love you and consider you their friend. Though why I have no idea. You are nothing more than a pain in our bottoms all the time," Elizabeth fussed.

"You love me as well." She could hear the pain in his voice and worried over it. "I do hurt badly and fear I will be a watery mess if I don't have some relief soon. Do you have a brew you could mix for me? I think sleep is what I need for now."

She knew as well as the man standing next to her, that sleep would not heal him. But she had Ephrae, Elvar's lady wife, brew him something a little stronger than she would for most. As soon as it was warm enough for him to take down, the king drained the cup with a thanks. Within minutes he was snoring soundly.

It took them nearly five hours to get him stitched back together. His leg was the worst off, needing her to put nearly a hundred small knotted threads in it after they'd scrubbed it clean of the dark waters. She could only surmise that the monster had been tainted himself and had poisoned the king when he'd cut him. But it was the wound to his belly that worried her more.

It wasn't deep or even long, but it had cut into his muscle and she'd had to stitch it three different times before she'd been able to make it hold. Then they'd bound him tightly, hoping it would keep him from moving and pulling her fine work out again. As she sat near the table and held his hand, Ephrae brought her a cup of some brew. First sip told her it was made of the lavender that she'd seen in the back yard.

"He will live?" Ephrae asked. She nodded at her and smiled. "The king, he has saved the champion, has he not? By killing that monster, he has helped the champion as we could not."

"I hope so." She'd forgotten about Aurora until then. And with remembering her, she also remembered the girl had his blood. Elizabeth wondered how she was fairing right now or if she'd felt him at all. "I should contact her. I need to…with the monster dead, mayhap I can speak to her again."

She started to get up, then sat down. Elizabeth eyed the tea and then the woman. Ephrae laughed. "There is nothing but tea in your cup, my lady. I would never give you something without you knowing. You could make me into something that I would not like so I would never do such a thing to one such as yourself. What you are feeling, I think, it's from your fear and hard work. Mayhap you should have s nap yourself. The champion will be all right now that the king has killed the beast." Elizabeth sat down hard and closed her eyes.

"I did it before to someone and I've regretted it for all this time. Aurora, I did it to her and she cut us both to ribbons for it." Her body, exhausted beyond anything she'd ever felt before, was becoming too heavy for her. Her head nodded forward twice before she finally looked at Ephrae. "I need to close my eyes. Will you kindly call my name, should he wake before me?"

"I shall." Or that's what she thought she said to her as Elizabeth simply closed her eyes and let the darkness take her.

Elizabeth opened her eyes and had to sit very still until her mind caught up with where she was. It wasn't a room she knew and her heart pounded hard in her chest until she remembered the king. Standing up slowly, so as not to creak the chair she'd been in or her tired bones, she checked his color against the roaring fire and the coolness of his skin. When he put his hand over hers, she stared into his drugged eyes.

"You will contact her now?" he asked.

Elizabeth nodded and told him in the same whispery tone he'd used, that she would now. "Tell her that I'm fine. Tell her...tell her it was only practice for when she gets here. That now that I've done the hard work for her, she should get her bottom up and working again."

"I will." Elizabeth moved out of the house before he could see her tears. He would live. And not only that, so would the girl. Had she died or been too terribly hurt, the king would have told her. She, too would have felt it, like she had his pain. But unlike Aurora, Elizabeth had seen his wounds and how he had begged to be put out. It would be a memory that would haunt her for the rest of her days and then some.

She sat near the tree in the big yard and reached out for Illuminaria first. She answered almost immediately and asked after her mate. Elizabeth assured her he was doing well. "It was scary, if you want to know the truth of it at first. Then he woke this morn, ordering me about as if it were a normal day for him."

"That sounds so like him. I felt his pain and knew that he'd been harmed. But I could not come to him or you. The mountain is a place I can't breach." Elizabeth had thought for a while now that she could not come here for one of two reasons. She simply didn't want to or it was because her body was here. Elizabeth would bet it was the latter of the two. *"When I felt the pain, I knew not if it was his or the champion's at first. I still am not...it took a great deal out of me when I came to see you. And when she was hurt, it felt as if my body would never wake."*

"I was going to go to her. Would you be able to come as well?" Elizabeth asked.

Illuminaria told her no, she didn't have the strength as yet. *"Then I will tell her that you come soon, shall I?"* Elizabeth said.

"Thank you. I would like that." Elizabeth stood up and walked to her home as Illuminaria continued. *"I have something for her as well. I have…it It's hidden in my gardens for her and when she is able to get the lake moving again, the lady of the lake, or someone will give it to her."*

"She is a very good champion, better than I was." Illuminaria told her she was wrong. *"Nay, I'm right. Aurora has done more in the small amount of time she had been here than I have done in all my lifetime. The quests would have…something would have kept me from my task I think. Also, I think the quests would not have been completed but for her. She is the bravest person I know."*

"I, as well. I hope before this is finished I can wrap my arms around her, if only for a moment or two. And because of her, I'm becoming stronger all the time, but not enough yet to touch her." Elizabeth knew that the queen could enjoy a cup of tea with her, had seen her pick a flower in a garden, but when she was with the champion, she could not touch. Again she had a feeling it had more to do with magic of the champion than it did with the queen's ability to do as she wished. *"When you see her, please tell her that I think of her often and that I thank her for doing this. You, too Miss Beth. I thank you so very much, every day for you and your wisdom. And for caring for my love. Envir would not have made it had it not been for your love of us both. You are a true friend to me,"* Illuminaria said.

Elizabeth told her that she loved her as well and the connection closed. Settling into a comfortable position, she pulled her basket of herbs and pots onto her lap. Aurora might not be hurt, but she had a feeling that she might be. Elizabeth had no idea what she'd see when she got there. She'd leave Aurora's merry men with enough things to set her to rights. As she closed her eyes and thought of the young woman, she could feel her pain and worried over it. Then she realized that it wasn't hers, but that of the king. Aurora was feeling the king's pain as though it was hers. It was their shared blood, and for a moment, she wondered if the king was tasting a little of it as well. Moving to the ring the faeries had helped her set up all those many years ago, she placed the single bud in the circle and willed herself to the child.

The darkness of the night startled her. She had no idea why she'd thought it would be bright where Aurora was, but she knew that it was dark where she was and it only stood to reason it would be there as well. The bright fire burning not far from where she'd ended up had her turning that way. The voices of the men, loud and laughing made her feel somewhat better. They would be very quiet if the champion was resting or at least she hoped they would. Pavel saw her first and stood to greet her. Elizabeth so liked the great lion.

"We were having a small celebration." He nodded to his right. "Aurora was telling us of a machine in her world that heats food in seconds and is only this big." He put out his hands to indicate about two feet wide. "And there is this food that she misses called corned popped. I should like to taste it, I was telling her."

"It's popcorn, and it's very good. With lots of butter and salt. The king and I have had it here. As for the microwave, I've seen them as well. Not that small, mind you but something much bigger." Elizabeth sat down on the log so that it would not make them think about how she wasn't there but in spirit. "I've not been to the other world in decades, for much more than a stop over to pick something up that was needed by the king. I would imagine things have gotten smaller in that amount of time. Everything has a tendency to get smaller after time."

"They have." Aurora nodded to her before continuing. "He is well, I take it. Hurt, I think, but well enough. He more than likely ordered you here. If he wasn't well, you wouldn't have left his side to come to me, would you, my lady? I could both murder him myself and hug him until he couldn't breathe for what has happened."

"I would rather be with you than him most of the time. He is a cantankerous man I want to slap." Aurora laughed, as did the men. "He is well. Hurt as you say, but well. There is a wound in his belly that worries me some but I think he will be fine in a few days. That is if I can get him to lie still long enough for his wound to tighten up a little."

"He will be fine. I'm working what magic I can from here." Aurora lifted her shirt and there was the same wound on her as on the king. It was healing, as the king's was, but Elizabeth was surprised at how much it had healed in the small amount of time she'd been here. "The wounds he had on his leg and arm have disappeared I think, because mine are all but gone as well. This one is much smaller than it was. The earth is healing us both."

Elizabeth looked at what she had assumed was a blanket over Aurora's legs. Instead it was soil and it was moving over her. As she watched the earth moved over her legs in a waterfall fashion so that it made its way to the earth again at each turn. It was something that she knew the young woman could do, call upon the earth to help her. But this looked as if it was helping her in ways that not even Elizabeth would have guessed. It was as if it were bathing her in their magic. Aurora laughed and she looked at her.

"It's revitalizing itself, it told me. Using very little of my magic to take with it when it takes some of my pain...or the king's pain away. Almost as soon, as I was laid here, the earth moved up and over me as if it knew what it was doing. I suppose in a way it did." Elizabeth nodded unsure what to think. "And it's healing the king, too. His wounds will...we are healing the king."

"I'm amazed at this. I mean...had you asked me, I would have said that you can gain some strength from the earth, but to have it working this way is something I've never seen before. This only goes to prove what I've been saying all along. You are a good deal stronger than me." Aurora smiled at her but said nothing. She watched her closely before speaking. Elizabeth felt her mind in sort of jumble. The things this girl could do would...she could move mountains, should she chose so, Elizabeth thought and so much more.

"Are you going to lose it, Miss Beth? You're not going to freak out on me are you?" The soil moved again, as if to reach out to her and she watched it. Elizabeth had a feeling if she wasn't all right, the soil would pull her down under it to heal her as well. She shivered at the thought. "Miss Beth? Are you okay?"

"I am well. I think. I've no idea what *freak out* even means, but I would not do something with such a dreadful name." Aurora laughed again. "I will admit that I am a little in awe of this. How do you know this is caring for the king as well? And that...you said you were put here and it started to heal you. I should like to know, how is it that you have such a connection to the earth, my child?"

"I really don't know. As I said, as soon as I sat down, it started to cover me. At first I was kind of worried it was going to bury me alive but it only moved over my bare skin. And where it couldn't get to my skin, it moved under my pant legs until it could. Trianam cut them away so it would work faster when we realized what it was trying to do." Elizabeth nodded again, feeling somewhat overwhelmed by it all. "The king, he'll be stronger for it, I think. Just as I am," Aurora said.

"Yes, I've no doubt that you both will gain a great deal from this. The earth will, as well. I've never seen such a thing and I can't wait to tell his lordship. He will be most impressed." Aurora snorted and Elizabeth smiled. "He will pretend he is not, but I think he will be all the same. You are going to save us, Aurora, despite ourselves."

CHAPTER 6

The removal of the snow was slow going. First it had to be boiled until it was nothing but clear water. Then cooled. The cooling took less time than she thought it might, as the air around them was still very cold. Aurora had asked the sun to hold off for a little while longer until she could make sure there would be no harm to anything when the snow was melted.

The bowls, as Vildar had been calling them, had worked perfectly after a few tweaks. The spout at the rear had turned out not to be a good idea because the person pushing the bowl around would get their boots soaked in mud. A simple moving of the bowl and spout to the side made things much better.

"We have enough water now to water every tree from here to the mountain." As much as Trianam sounded upset with the work, Aurora knew that he, like the others, was enjoying the task. It was hard work, but it was better than sitting around waiting for something to happen. Even after the second day, Aurora was moving around a little better and wondered how the king was doing.

"The water of the lake is what worries me. It's solid," she said. Trianam nodded and looked in the direction of the trees standing guard over it. "We can get rid of all this stuff but without the lake to sustain the area, I'm worried that nothing will grow here. Even after we put it in the ground."

"Have you talked to the lady of the lake? To see what she can do?" he asked. She told him she was sort of afraid to. "Aye. I can see that. We've nothing better to do than to dig up hard snow that will be for naught should we get it all done. Having the information would seem trivial to that sort of task. I, meself would have seen to that quickly, but then I'm only the lowly tool that you brought along. You just keep doing what you've been up to and we'll muddle through it all."

"I don't care for you overly much right now." He only grinned at her. "I'll talk to her tonight. Once we get the—"

"Ye'll go now, my lady. It has you worrying mightily and that's not good for the lot of us. Makes you...makes you a thing you call cranky. Go. Ask her what we're to do once we have the snow removed and cleaned. I've a need for a nice warm day, meself." She stuck her tongue out at him as she moved away. "Yes. That is a good way to start this. Make her think you'd be nothing more than a child. If you were my child, I'd paddle you hard, I would."

She knew that he would never raise a hand to his child. And what's more, the child would not be spoiled about it either. Trianam would be firm and quiet in the ruling of his child, but he would never scream and yell at him. He would be a good father and a great role model to his children.

Aurora was actually kind of afraid of the answer the lady of the lake was going to give her. The lake had been frozen for a lot longer than the flowers had guessed. Five years would have been about the length of time it would've taken for the new little bud to have become aware, she'd thought and now...well, Aurora and the rest of them had an idea the lake had been like this for many decades. As she came to the stand of trees, she put her hand on the first one she saw. It was warmer than it had been, and greeted her cheerfully.

"We are in anticipation of you getting things readied for us. The earth talks of nothing but how the champion and her men are working tirelessly to make our land whole again." Aurora told her that she was trying. "You are doing well, my lady. What is it I can do for you this fine day?"

"I've come to talk to the lady of the lake, or to see if I can talk to her. How are the waterways faring?" There was no answer for several seconds and Aurora knew that things were bad. "I know there's no life in her. It worries me that she is so quiet now."

"I have spoken to the water beneath us. The one we reach with our...taproot as you called it. She said there could be life for the lake, but she is stubbornly holding onto her icy grave. The waterways aren't as tainted as they could have been but she won't help us." Aurora asked her what she meant. "She has no desire to let go of the cold, so that life can become hers again. The lady of the lake is saying that it 'tis a trick, and that once she is warmed again, the sun will hide its warmth from her, and she will be cold once again. She has no desire to be free only to be frozen again."

Aurora tried to think what that would mean. "You mean she's afraid that the monster will chill her again? I assure you, that's not going to happen. The king has—"

"Oh no, my lady. She knows he is gone forever. We have all felt his death and are happy for it. She never wants to be frozen over again." The tree shivered enough that snow, what little there was on her, drifted down over the ground and Aurora. "She is being most stubborn as I've said. Her thinking and her demands are that she never be cold again. And that is not fair to the rest of us."

Aurora agreed with her and walked to the lake. She could talk to her. It drained her a great deal to try and speak to the frozen waterways but right now she figured it was talk to her, maybe she could reason with her or whatever they were doing was going to be for nothing. Just as Trianam had said. Clearing off the thick snow with her gloved hand, Aurora laid her bare fingers over the water and reached deeply.

"I wish to speak to you, if you please." The lake warmed ever so slightly under her fingers. Not enough to melt much but enough to know that she'd heard Aurora and nothing more. "So you can warm up a little, only chose not to. That's not what I need from you. I would wish that you'd start to thaw now, if you are able. It's imperative to the—"

"I don't care what you need. I've been thusly for too long to care should you threaten me with the king." Well, that wasn't going to work, thought Aurora. "There is no reason for me to become warm only to be hardened again over and over. There is nothing in my waterways that would need me to become soft again so I don't wish it. What good would it do me should I thaw and someone thinks to kill me again? Nothing. I rule my own ways, you don't. I care not who you say you are."

"But I do. And I'm going to have to demand that you warm up. There isn't just you involved in this, but a lot of other creatures as well. Even the trees, that have been guarding you, are in need of your water. I need for—"

"I won't do this." Aurora was knocked back on her butt and sat there. She'd just been yelled at by water. And nicely done as well. As she stood up, one of the trees bent nearly double. Aurora walked to it, and was startled to hear a male voice as it spoke to her.

"My lady, if I may suggest, perhaps it would be best if we talked to her." She asked him why. "She is...I would say she is in the wrong, but I do believe you are aware of that. The lady of this waterway has been...the frozen king abused her badly when she was only but a puddle in the eyes of ground."

"You mean that she wasn't this big when this place was made?" He shook his mighty limbs as an answer. "What did he do to her? You said the self-proclaimed frozen king abused her, how did he do that?"

"When we were but saplings, he didn't try to rule. It was said that he was...he was a goodly man and the king would not listen to him. We have since found out his ravings were not as he said, but that of a madman set on taking what didn't belong to him." Aurora knew that and waited. "Then when he returned after many days of seeing the king, he proclaimed to the animals and anything else of the plan to be a ruler of a plot of land, this land, and the gardens of the queen. He said that the king made it so."

"He thought to give him a bit of land he could own, not an entire region that he would kill. And he has, as you know." The tree told her that he knew this as well. "I'm sorry. What were you telling me about the abuse? I need to know all of it if I'm to help her to see reason."

"I can tell you what we all know, my lady. It's a sad and very terrible tale, I'm a feared. She was but a puddle and he said he would like for her to be bigger. Every day he'd come by and say that she wasn't large enough, that her waters were not to his liking. And daily she would work harder in making her waters as he had requested. Deeper, too deep at times, to let any of the animals grow and live there. Nothing could live in the deepness as it was cold well below the earth on which we stand even now. When it became apparent to us she would take over the region with her shores, we stood around her and would not let her take any more ground. It was...she is deeper than anything you can imagine, my lady, and she would have been wider had it not been for us standing guard." Aurora looked around the area as the tree continued his story. "When she would not be able to take more ground, the frozen king said he would cut us down, burn us where we stood. But he didn't. It was much too much effort, so he only growled and cursed at us. Still we stand."

So they weren't guarding her as she'd originally thought. Riding over this lake, she could see that it was huge, not ocean-huge but more than any lake that she'd ever seen in all her life. Sitting down, Aurora leaned her back against the tree and continued talking to him.

"So what would you say to her? I mean, if she is unhappy that she'll have to freeze over for only a short amount of time yearly, then perhaps we can come to some kind of agreement. She won't have to be frozen solid, as she is now. Animals and other things will still live beneath the ice, but it will be cold and there will always be a thaw now." Aurora heard the tree sigh heavily behind her. "I don't know what to do other than that. There has to be seasons. You've seen firsthand what not having them can do for a region."

"But that is not all that he did to her." His voice was low and full of pain. So much so that Aurora turned to look up at him. "He poisoned her so that he could be formed."

"He made his body from her icy depths?" The tree told her that he had, daily came to her and dove in and came up with more and more ice. "But that won't happen again. Things are going to be back to normal...well, as normal as we can make them. She needs to see reason. The earth here needs her, too."

"She is most angry, my lady champion. But we will talk with her for you. See if we, those who kept her safe, can reason with her some."

Aurora made her way back to where Trianam was when she had the story. There was probably more, but she had to get away for a little bit in order to calm her temper. As soon as she saw her friend, she drew her sword and told him to stand ready.

"No," he said. She swiped her blade at him to make him see that she wasn't taking no for an answer. "I won't fight you, or be your punching bag, whatever that may be, so that you can work out your problems. As you have said to me before, we don't fight out of anger, we speak of it. Speak to me of what ails you," Trianam said.

"You've done it to me often enough. Get your stupid sword out and fight me. Or so help me, I will hurt you." He asked her if that would make her feel better. "I think so. I really do."

When he did nothing more than try to avoid her blade, she thought about making him mad verbally. Calling him names only made him laugh, and when she talked about how useless he was to her, he only laughed harder. It wasn't until she brought up his lady wife that he started to get mad.

"What do you think your wife is doing right now? Huh? Do you think she's realizing that she no longer needs you?" Aurora taunted.

He told her to behave herself. "No. I want to tell you what I think your wife is doing. Do you suppose that she's lazing about, having someone else take care of your son? Or do you suppose that she is— Oof."

Trianam had her down on her back and his blade at her throat before she could say more. Struggling only made him dig the knife into her throat, but he never drew blood. When she tired herself out, she lay there looking up at him, and let the tears flow.

"He hurt her. Made her into a monster as bad as he was. Freezing her water and killing the few animals and creatures left in her body was all she could do to save herself and the trees around her." He asked her if she was going to be all right. "I don't know. She's so afraid to thaw and one of us asks her to...ask her to... Trianam, he poisoned her water when she was deep enough for the water in the darkness to be cold enough to make him. Then he used her water to freeze even the smallest of creatures, tossing them into her depths and he had her bring them to the deep where they faced a watery grave, frozen as he was. Her heart began to chill, then freeze until she was nothing more than water without a purpose."

"So she thinks that if she no longer lets anything into her heart, then nothing more can hurt her?" She nodded. "Then what will we do?"

"I don't know. I really don't," Aurora said. He moved off her and she curled to her side, lying still. "If we can't get her to open up for us. Then everything here will starve. Even the trees. Because once the warmness of summer comes, there will be nothing to keep everything from dying again."

~~~

Envir watched the men putting together the barn. He hadn't been helping as much as getting in the way, his injuries, while healed, were not allowing him to move or lift much. So now he watched. And he learned. Today they were putting the roof on and climbed up and down the ladders as easily as he shifted from man to dragon. He looked over at his namesake when he stood beside him.

Young Envir watched them as he did. Every move he made, the boy did as well. When Envir sat down and leaned back on his hands, the boy tried his best to stretch his legs out the length of Envir's and he had to hide a smile. There was a little hero worship there, and Envir kind of liked it.

"You will be as long legged and strong as your father soon enough, young man," the king said. He nodded and the boy smiled up at him. In the last several days, the boy had lost his front teeth and it gave him a cute lisp as well. "What do you think of the barn they raise? Will it be big enough to hold all that you need come winter?"

"Aye, it will. Father said it will hold all that we hold dear because it will keep us from starving come winter. I've met her," his namesake said. It took Envir a second or two to realize he'd meant Aurora. The quick change of subject, Envir had gotten used to. The boy was like a bullet being fired from a gun when he did it. "She is most beautiful, do you not think so my lord?"

Envir smiled but only nodded. He'd been told by the boy's father that he had spoken of nothing but the young champion since their meeting. Elvar said he had plans to marry the young miss and to have a house in the mountains beside him.

"The champion is most beautiful, young Envir. And she is hard, too. Did you know that she has killed for me? And even been hurt badly enough that I thought her to die?" He nodded. Everyone had heard the stories about his champion. "I worry that when she comes here, that she will be so tired that she will only want to rest and not be bothered," Envir told the boy.

"I shan't bother her, my lord. I will care for her as my father does my own blessed mother. She won't want for anything." Envir nodded and glanced in the direction of his own wife, almost letting himself feel sorry for his own loss of love. "I wish to ask you for her hand in marriage. I will care for her as you have," the boy said.

"You will?" the boy nodded solemnly. "And what do you think she'd say about marrying you, my good man? Do you think that she'd...well, she is much older than you. I believe her to be as old as your own mother."

"It matters not. I will be of her age soon, too." Envir wondered if the boy really thought that, or was it wishful thinking on his part. "Is she to live forever, my lord? As you do and the Lady Elizabeth?"

"Yes. She's going to be pretty upset about that when I tell her too. She thinks...I don't know if she still thinks it or not, but she believes she might go back to the other world when she has completed her tasks here. Your own mother will miss you when you leave I think."

"I could take her with me." Envir nodded. "And the rest of my family. I have five brothers now, counting the one that has yet to arrive. They'll come with me as well.

My mother with my father too. We shall be a family there."

"And what of your uncles and aunts? Do you think them to come along too?" Young Envir nodded, but didn't look so sure now. "And your grandmother and grandfather. They are old, do you suppose they'd want to make the move as well with you? Otherwise, you'll need to leave them behind."

"They will need to come as well." Young Envir looked out over the barn that was nearly roofed. "I shall need a house as big as the barn, I believe. I have only a few coins to make her a house. 'Twill be a great amount to house so many, you think, my lord?"

"It will be. Housing is expensive in the other world. And there will be no one to help you build it like there is here. You'll be leaving them all behind to follow your dream of marrying my champion." Young Envir nodded but said no more. Envir didn't either. He was content to watch and wait.

"Food too would be costly I think," the boy said finally. Envir said nothing. "I could hunt daily, but my father has not allowed me to fire a weapon so it might be a while before I can provide for her."

"You can't hunt in her world as you do here. And her world has no magic." That shocked the young man into standing up and looking at him as if he'd...well, become a dragon. "I can't be my dragon there either. Should you want me to come for a visit. There are no trees to chop down, no hunting in the cities, and there is nowhere for a young man newly starting out with a wife and a huge family to grow a garden either. You will need to find yourself a job that pays well to even make the monthly bills."

"Bills come due monthly?" Envir was having a hard time fighting his laughter. It was just too much fun to tease the boy into realizing that his true love was going to be expensive even if she did want to take him on. "I can't afford that. I only get one coin a month to cover my own...what sort of expenses is your champion going to have?"

She was no longer his true love, but his champion now. Envir sat up and looked around. "Well, there will be her haircuts, clothing that will need to be cleaned by a professional. They call them dry cleaners. I've no idea how that is to work. Then her nails will need to be done weekly as well as shopping. Women do love to shop in the other world." Young Envir sat down as he continued. "Then there will be her car, as well as your own. I have told you of such a thing, haven't I?"

"Aye, you did." He sounded so dejected that Envir wanted to hold him on his lap until he felt better. "Having a wife is surely expensive, isn't it my lord?"

"It is. It is. But, you'll love her and not wonder where your money goes when she loses it while out shopping." Young Envir shook his head, saying that she'd never lose money. "She would there. There is a different set of things going on there that we don't have here. There will be days when she will wish to have luncheons with her friends. As well as you will need to buy her flowers, as they aren't readily available as they are here. Children too, might come along and then they would be an added expense to your monthly bills. And Aurora will need you to get her a gift for each child that she bares you. More for a boy child. I could go on about how she would need new shoes with every shirt and dress she buys as well as—"

"My lord?" Envir nodded. "I've thought about it, and I think you are correct in saying that she and I will not suit."

"I never said you would never suit, I was only pointing out that she might need more than your one coin a week can provide." Young Envir nodded and looked out over the barn where his father was hammering and his mother was helping set up lunch for them all. "You might be very happy with her as your bride," the king said.

"Nay, I won't. Leaving here would...it would hurt my mother, I think. And my grandparents are very old. The change would hurt their hearts I think. I know 't'would mine." Envir said nothing again, letting the boy come to his own answers. "Mayhap I will remain a boy for a bit longer and wait for someone...a bride from here to care for. She won't know of things such as nails being done. Though why she would want to have the nails done is beyond me. Do you suppose she likes them painted before they are hammered in the wall or after?"

"I'm sure after." Envir watched the boy nod then run off. He was nearly to the barn when Envir stood up. He saw Miss Beth behind him, holding her hand over her mouth with great tears at her cheeks. Her mirth made his own harder to contain.

"She would have talked to him, as well but I would not have been privileged to see what you think of women as you told him." He nodded and walked toward her. "You are resting well, my lord? Not straining yourself overly much talking nonsense to a young boy?"

"Nay, I was in the way of them. They still treat me as if I'm mortally wounded." He had been. The frozen king had hurt him badly and his belly still pained him some. "I've only been sitting here a bit, really. I was...would you walk with me for some time? I have a need to move again."

"Of course." She moved alongside him and he knew that she was keeping an eye on his movements. To be honest he was still sore and knew when the men had asked him to have a seat, they were doing so out of concern for him rather than him being in their way. As his strength returned, he knew that walking was the best thing for him. "I've heard from the trees. Aurora is having trouble with the lake there. The lady of the lake has decided she had no desire to thaw for her. I believe that my Aurora is going to try and reason with her a little more before she takes it...you said it once. Something about a cow. No. A bull," Miss Beth said.

"Take the bull by the horns. I have no idea what it means really, but I've heard it a great deal." He thought about the lake. "Is there a reason for this stubbornness? And so you know, that is something I've come to enjoy out of both my champions, but not my waterways."

"She is not happy either, I guess." Miss Beth smiled at him. "She is working through it however. She and the lake have had numerous conversations and I'm not sure who has come out the top. Even Trianam has spoken to the lake as well and the trees have said it's funny to watch a grown man leaning into a bed of ice and yelling at it. I do believe I'd pay real money to see that." So would Envir. He would love to see a great many things that Aurora and her men were doing and found himself excited about how close they were to him.

"She will figure it out. And if she needs us, she will ask." He had come to realize while he'd been lying in the bed recuperating, that this champion might well be the very thing he needed as well as his world. Not that he didn't already know it, but it was more personal to him now. "I'm both looking forward to me coming to me and not at the same time. The few times that we have talked, I've been...it's been business talk and nothing personal. Do you suppose that she will not like me much?"

When she didn't answer him, Envir stopped to look at her. And was shocked to find her so far behind him. He started to ask her if he'd been walking too fast, again when she stormed at him as if she meant to hit him. As soon as her hand smacked across his cheek, he stood there stunned to see her walking away from him.

"Miss Beth have I—" She turned back to him and started walking hard again. Envir took several steps back, fearful that she meant him harm again. There was a look in her eye that frankly scared him and not just a little either.

"Of all the...what is wrong with you? Did you perhaps hit your head and I missed it looking you over when that monster laid you out so recently? Are you addled, as I've heard you ask the champion on many occasion?" He wasn't sure what to say to her in her anger. "Do I think she'll like you, you ask me? What gave you...you know what? I don't care where you got that foolish notion. For one minute did you think...? No, you have not thought. I could just hit you again, I'm so angry with you."

"Please don't." He wasn't sure what had made her so angry, but he was enjoying it. "I should like a reason that you have hit your king."

He could see the moment that she realized what she'd done. And when she dropped to the ground, her body almost one with the dirt beneath her, he had to laugh. She was such a joy and he might have missed it, should he have stayed the king he'd been. He reached down to help her up and had to stifle a laugh, or perhaps be injured again.

"Get up, if you please. I've a mind to talk to you and I don't wish to do so with your backside staring at me in the face." He laughed again when she growled low. "Miss Beth, I'm not angry. I've come to realize that life is much too short to be angry all the time. I want to...I will be free of the moods I've been in until now. And I know that I've been morose as well, something that I work daily to bring myself out of."

"You aren't going to run me through? It's what I deserve. Hitting the king, I know is a punishment of death. I would do it to anyone who would dare do such a thing. And here I am, smacking you upside the head as I should do to my son more often. But you anger me so when you say things like that." She looked up at him, still on her knees. "Sire, you can't believe that she would not love you as everyone does. I know she angers you so, but you...you do seem to have a better grip on your own sadness."

"I doubt very much that everyone loves me, Miss Beth but I do thank you for that. As for my sadness, yes, I have it. It has not lessened overly much but I am...I would suppose you could say that I'm dealing with it in a healthier way." He helped her stand. "Now, tell me about the pots she had to make to boil the snow. Did the things we sent her, they have helped?"

"She had the men that work with her, Vildar the iron man, and Markard his assistant, fashion large bowls from the plates of iron you sent. The glass that was sent was used just as Elvar had shown us in making a bright hot fire with the opals we were able to take to her. Did you know the headache powders were used for just that? Her head had been hurt by the monster." He had known that she'd been hurt and was glad that something had worked out for her. "They have two large pots that are heated as they move. Working in two men teams, they fill the pots with the snow and let it trickle out of the side gently as they moved around the fields. It waters the soil I am to understand. It's slow work, my lord, and I wonder if they will ever get it all done."

"They will." He knew that she would. "This lake she is having issues with. Is there something that Ox might do for her? He has a great number of things he can do. Perhaps we should let him know of her difficulties," Envir said.

"I'd say that would be a good idea." They walked for a bit longer and she paused by one of the gardens he'd help put in. "Things are growing much faster this year. Is it the fertilizer you have been working with?"

"I believe so. I've heard from Genese about what they are dealing with at the Castle too. More than enough, she said, to fertilize every blade of grass that ever comes above ground." He laughed. "Venitice is doing a splendid job as well, making sure that the townspeople are doing what they should and helping each other as well. And I heard that Venitice's wife is breeding. And they are all well."

"Yes. Sophiand is as well. But she is much further along, I'm told. It's said that Karrah is about to bust with happiness and that no man can come near him without hearing how he is going to be a father." Envir had heard that as well. But as he sat down, he closed his eyes briefly to let the pain of walking settle. "You should be resting more, not gallivanting about the fields like you have not a care in the world. I know you have been told this several times, but you, as your champion is, are a very stubborn man," Miss Beth fussed.

"I don't wish to die." She sat down beside him and he reached for her hand. "I have...I know that I wished it for so long, but I do no longer. I want to make the world, this world a better place for my people and their families as well. Will you help me?"

"I will do anything for you, and you know it." He nodded and sat there holding onto her hand, and her warmth. "Envir, what has happened to you?"

"I nearly died. I know that. Even then I knew I was as close to death as any man or dragon could ever be, and I didn't care for the feeling. There is so much I can do. Things that my love and I talked about that need to be...I should like to make them come to fruition. I want to make this place a place of peace and happiness. I know it will never be perfect, as king, I know that now. But I should like to make it a home for us all. A place we can be safe and prosper as well."

"I will be honored to help you." He nodded. "Now, go back to your bed and rest. I have bread rising on the hearth, and there is all manner of jellies that I must fix before it goes bad. Winter will be upon us before we know it."

"Yes it will." As he made his way back to the little cabin he'd made for himself, he reached out to Ox and let him know what was happening in his gardens. He told him he'd look into it and get back to him. There were things afoot he said that he didn't fully understand. Thanking him, Envir lay down and closed his eyes. He smiled, thinking that Aurora was going to come home to him soon.

CHAPTER 7

The snow was gone. Not all of it, but enough that they could see grasses beginning to spring up and the trees around the area were finally sprouting their buds. It was late in the year for them of course, but they'd do fine, Aurora had told him. Trianam looked at her now as she held the plow that was currently making a long furrow in the newly formed garden. She was a wonder, she was.

"Shall I have a turn?" he asked.

She told him to get his own plow and he watched her a bit more. They had three of them now, the large pots that had served them so well had been cut down and turned into the large earth movers for their use.

Uerthe was pulling one of the other plows. The dirt didn't stand a chance to stay where it was. As the furrows were opened, he and Vildar would go behind her and drop seeds into the land. After they finished a row, then Markard and Pavel would come behind them and cover it up. As soon as the earth covered the tiny seeds or plants, then Aurora would go behind them still and touch the earth to beg for their help in getting the seedlings a good start. It was a system that was working well for them. He looked over at the large garden they had already planted.

He just hoped that someone would be able to enjoy it before it dried up.

Corn was popping its tasseled heads up now. Even the beans that had been planted were now creeping up the long lines of twine that he'd fashioned for them to run along. Pavel had been very helpful in trying to figure out a pattern to the madness that was gardening, and now there were things growing side by side, helping each other along. Corn would serve to hold up the cucumbers and the tomatoes were helping the seeds of potatoes get more sun as they were planted in the same hole. Even the trees that they'd planted seemed to have some artistry behind them.

Plums were near apples, the colors so brilliant it was almost painful to watch when the wind caught it just right. Some of the other fruits had yet to be named, that Aurora and Mykaal had made were coming along nicely as well. Just last night, they'd had trout from a nearby stream with candied pears and peaches for evening meal. Something that Aurora had suggested, but had not a clue how to cook. The fresh green beans had been grilled as well, having a taste he'd grown quite fond of even after the first bite. Watching her now made him wonder, and not for the first time what sort of life she'd had in her other world.

When she stopped moving down the row and stared off to the trees, he handed the plow he'd only just hooked up, over to Zapps. There was something afoot and he would not leave her alone to go to it. As they made their way to the lake again, Trianam felt his heart hurt for what had happened to it and wanted to find the frozen king and kill him himself.

"She is calling to me through the trees and the earth," Aurora said. He nodded but didn't take his hand off his sword. He had no way to fight water but he would be ready should she need him. "I don't know what it could be. I thought for sure she said she didn't want to talk to me ever again. Made that point perfectly clear, as a matter of fact."

Trianam knew that it had hurt her, the way that the lake wouldn't talk to her and when she had spoken, it was with meanness in her heart and her words. He was also pained because, she had been hurt so badly as well when the lake had moved her ice in a way that had thrown Aurora back hard against one of the nine trees surrounding it. The frozen king would have much to answer for, if he were still alive. But again, if he were, they'd not know of this abuse. As they made their way to the water, Trianam could see that the trees around it had branched out, their green reaching high in the sky. It was indeed a beautiful sight to behold. And to realize he'd been a part of it.

"They told me they were no longer going to wait on her," the champion said. He could see that. The trees were greening up much like the rest of the world here was. He started to ask Aurora if she knew if they'd live or not, but she answered him before he could. "I hope that their roots are deep enough to sustain them. And that I hope I can get waterways to open around the gardens we're planting." She put her hand on the icy water and looked up at him. Her expression was unreadable to him, her mouth set in a smile but her eye twinkled in a bit of anger.

"You've a strange look upon your face. What is it? She yelling at you again?" Aurora shook her head and smiled bigger. "I don't think I want to know," Trianam muttered.

"Do you remember me telling you about Ox, the merfish king?" He nodded thinking that would be a sight to see. Half man and half fish. He nodded again. "Apparently he's been talking to the lake. And she's none too happy about it. She is of course blaming me for it. They are arguing...I think he's not really helping the situation."

"She blames you then?" Aurora nodded. "Have you told her that should she have done the right thing in the first place, we'd not have to...? How did he know? The king told him you think? You think he has been begging for his help on your behalf then?"

"I would imagine so." She sat on the ice and he had an urge to tell her she would get sick. The only place that wasn't sweltering hot was this place and it was as cold as...well, ice he supposed. Laughing slightly at his own joke, he sat as well but on the nice grasses that had come up and not the cold of the lake. "Tell me what she is yelling at you about. And what is he saying that has the lady so upset, if you please. I've a need for a good tale."

"I don't think she's going to do it, Trianam. She is very mad at us all." Aurora looked at him and he could see that she was fighting something and he had an idea it was her anger. But she looked as calm as well, as if she had not a worry in the world. "I've an idea. What if we cook her?"

"Cook her?" Aurora nodded. "You don't mean to set a fire under her, do you? I think there is not a pot big enough to hold all of her. And the trees have told you, she is deeper than she is wide. That is a powerful amount of water."

"I'm going to talk to Ox." He nodded and watched her get up off the icy stone of water and move to the grasses.

She stayed close enough to the water to touch it but he knew she was only using it as a connection and not talking to the lake too. As she lay there, he watched the area.

There were no animals out to play this time of day. At any time of day or night as a matter of fact. There were no birds singing their songs, no crickets chirping in the evening light either. He missed the firelights, or *fire flies* as Aurora called them, as well as the marvinrem and their mates. Everything here was dead. Long dead and nothing to replace them. Nothing could survive the cold and had simply died, frozen or starved when there was nothing for them to eat or a place to get warmed.

Had it not been for the king sending them meat that had been cured, and other things that kept them warm, they too might have been dead before they could get rid of the snow that had been on the ground longer than he'd been born. Trianam looked around when he heard a noise he'd never heard before. It sounded like the clacking of a great many swords. Men screaming their battle cries. Even the sounds of great stones being felled to the earth echoed around them. He stood up just as Pavel came to him as a great bear, his body coming fast even for his enormous size. As soon as he drew his sword, he saw that the Rismak were coming too. He wondered what was going on and took a step to Aurora to warn her when she sat up and looked at him.

"Run, Trianam. Run for your life!" He had no idea why she wanted him to do that, but when his own wings grabbed him up in his great claws, he watched as the rest of them were caught up as well. Even Tholan and Zapps, great heavy men were in the claws of the beasts as they made their way far from where they had been. Pavel and his bear were the last to be picked up just as the lake exploded.

~~~

Aurora watched the water make its way over the land. Great chunks of ice, some as big as a small car, tumbled down the hill where they had landed. Broken branches, even whole trees were tossed up from the grounds as the lake had a hissy fit of major proportions. Nothing within a football field of space looked as if it has been able to survive the blast.

She was glad now that they had planted the seeds and seedlings so deep or they might have been lost in the flood. The trees, young yet, would be all right as they were still a good mile away. As things settled back down, the water receded more and more, they made their way down the mountain that they'd been waiting on, careful of the great amount of mud that seemed to coat everything.

"What the blazes happened?" She really didn't know and said as much to Markard when he asked. "The water just...ice chunks as big as me...what did you do?"

"I did nothing. Her anger did this. Like you, I heard it start to break up and the earth told me to run to safety. I don't know what we would have done had I not been touching it." She was just sliding to a stop near the circle of trees, when the rest of them came to a stop as well. "I'm not sure what happened, but she was very mad. Ox is the one that was talking to her. He must've really upset her to have made her boil up like she did. When I talk to him I'm going to tell him just how I feel about him putting my friends at risk like he did. Stupid man. I wonder if they all think because they're in charge, they can bellow like they do."

She'd been terrified at first and knew that her wings, Uerthe, had been afraid for her, too. As soon as she'd told him what she felt, he told her to get to higher ground and he was bringing the rest. She'd not had any idea that water could come up so high or do so much damage when it did. Aurora shivered when she thought about them being at ground zero.

The circle of trees had gotten the worst of it. All nine of them had been broken low enough that she was sure that they might never recover. And Aurora thought that was bad enough. The grass that had been around it was now covered in the thick sauce-like mud and she moved to see if she could save it, but there was so much of it that she knew that those losses were great, as well. There were no grass seeds to replace them.

"Get the saws please, and cut the wood. We'll need to clean this mess up and then in some places, start over." Looking into the hole that had once been the lake she wondered if there would ever be enough water to fill in the deep hole. She looked at Trianam when he stood beside her. "She's gone. It wasn't ever my intentions for this to happen to her."

"'Tis not your fault. But I'd say that's a good estimation on her being gone." Aurora sat down in the mud, not caring a bit that she was being covered in the slime. "We've a bit of time, mistress. I think it would be best that you—"

"Do you think I killed her?" She looked up at him when he didn't answer her. "I know it was my quest to get this finished, but I never meant to make her so angry that she'd...well, do what she did. I'm not even counting how she might've hurt us with her temper tantrum." She could feel her anger rising and shook herself.

"Didn't you tell me that the Ox, this merfish person, was talking to her?" Aurora nodded and started to speak when Trianam continued. "And this man, he's a king you say, of the waters?"

"He is. But had I been able to solve this with her, he might not have stepped in." Trianam only cocked a brow at her. "Okay, I guess you're right. It was *her* that wasn't willing to help us. And her boss had to step in. But I don't have to like it."

"Nay, you don't. And it will bother you a bit more before you come to see that what you did was for the best. We've the lake thawed of sorts. Now we've a need to fill her back up. How do you say we do that, my lady champion?" He looked around, and she did as well. "No idea how we're to fill this hole up, in the event you're about to ask. And while we're about it, there be no fish to feed here. Do you suppose your Merfish....?"

The water burbled. It was a word she had never used before, but that is just what it did. Deep in the hole, there was perhaps a foot of murky mud and mire and it bubbled up like it was boiling. Aurora stood and readied herself to run with her men should the need arise. But as water began to fill the deep hole, she watched in awe as fish began to jump in the deepening pond.

In that moment, she knew that the next doorway had opened for them. She felt it as if she'd been standing next to it. The North Village was going to be their next quest. However, she also knew that the threads that locked the castle area away from this one was still closed off. And she thought that she knew why. There was nothing here to sustain even the grass as yet. Almost as soon as she thought of how she was going to clean this mess up, fat drops of rain began to fall on her and her men. Time to get to work, she supposed.

~~~

Envir was stunned. Okay, he supposed *stunned* wasn't a strong enough word, but he was *something*. When Ox said his name, he was sure it wasn't the first time. He assured the merking he was there and all right.

"You've quite a girl on your side there. Never would have...my goodness, you should have heard her pleading with the lady of the lake. Telling her what was to happen should she be as stubborn as she was being. It made me mad that the lake wasn't listening to reason. And stepping in, as I've known you to do on an occasion, well, I might have made matters worse, as I said before." Envir nodded then told him he understood. "Are you well, my friend? Have I hurt you in some way by coming to her aid?"

"No. never that. I'm thinking of...you had to destroy one of yours. I feel poorly for you." Ox assured him that wasn't what it was. "I know you said she brought it upon herself, but it could not have been easy to step in. I would have, but then I'm a tyrant. Or so I've been called before."

"You are a little on the bossy side. But then you've a lot on your shoulders, what with having a world to look after." Envir pointed out that the marking, too had a world to look after and Ox laughed before speaking. "'Tis not the same as what you have. I have the oceans and waterways, yes, but I have assigned others to help me out. The whales watch over their kind, as do certain other creatures and they report to me. You've no one like that, save your champion and she is cut off from you. Nay, 'tis not the same at all."

"I thank you for your help, Ox. Had you not stepped in, heavy handed or not, she might still be trying to reason with her. She will be home to me soon and I've not an idea what to say to her. Besides thanking her. I've this...well, no longer but this woman came to us untried, and untrained and she has managed to rid my world of things that I had no idea about." Ox said that he'd heard from the lakes. "I would imagine that they have a better story than I when it comes to her tales. She's been working harder than I ever dreamed a champion would have to coming here. And to find that the things she is taking care of makes me wonder if this world will ever be the same again." He heard Ox laughing and nearly joined him until he spoke.

"Do you need a tissue with your pity party, my lord?" Envir realized he was sort of whining and told his friend that he was fine. "I've spoken to her. Indirectly of course, in the form of the waterways that I've sent her. I could not leave things the way they were. And I'd had a notion she might be grateful for me helping her. Nay, not her. I believe her to be a great deal more like Lady Elizabeth than I'd first thought."

"She no doubt has pointed out the many things you did wrong. But I would guess she has a mess on her hands." He said that it more than likely was. "I had hoped she'd let me know how she is fairing. I shall have to annoy her again today just to make sure she is still on her toes. I think her to have a fine temper when it suits her," Envir said.

"Aye, she does. Had me...she brought me to task on the way things were done with me and the lady of the lake. Told me I should have had a better care for my words." Ox laughed again. "I swear to you, if she were not your champion, I should like to bring her to my deeps and make her one of mine. I've never seen a harder softer woman in my life."

That was a perfect description of the woman. She could be as hard as stone when she needed to be and soft in her heart when that was necessary, too. He thought about what she'd written him when thanking him for the books he'd been sending her. Envir thought about it now.

"My lord, don't get too lofty on the title. I'm thinking I should be nicer to you since you gave me something I will treasure for the rest of my life. But I won't be bowing down to you on bent knee and I wouldn't count on me calling you anything more than Kingy, either. But the book has always been a favorite of mine. And reading is a passion I've missed since coming here. Thank you so very much for this. As I've said, it will be something that I will keep close to my heart for all time. You're humbled servant, Aurora."

"Do you suppose she will need a break when she gets here? Or do you suppose she will need me to kick her around a bit to show her that I'm indeed her king." Ox laughed and so had he. "I was thinking of a feast of some sort, but I've a feeling she would harm me and a great many others when she sees it. Something simple and quiet would suit her more, I think. She is without a doubt very vocal when the mood suits," Envir said.

"I think that no matter what you do for her, she will appreciate it. But yes, the party would only embarrass her. She is more of a...I was going to say she's more of a quiet type, but that is not right either. The champion would be more at home, I think with a small token of your gratification and then left alone. But you do what you will. And I'm thinking of ways to repay her as well. With your permission, of course. She has done much to help my waterways. More than...well, more than I ever realized that I needed," Ox said.

"As you say, you do what you will, as will I my friend. And you no more need my permission than she would be to ask for it from either of us." They both agreed she was more of a do it and ask for forgiveness later sort of woman. "I must go to see to some things, my friend. Should you need either of us, we are here for you." Envir said.

"As I am for you, my dear friend." As the connection closed down, Envir wondered not for the first time, what Aurora would find when coming here. He'd been busy and his people were ready for the coming winter. What would she need to do when she came to his mountain? More he was sure than he could see, he was sure of it.

CHAPTER 8

Trianam knew they were going to have to work harder than they'd ever worked before in this region. The trees they'd planted, as well as all the rows of food were now being cleaned away of the mire by the rain, but there was still the devastation that the ice and water from the lake had done. The trees and the vegetation were just one of the things he could see that needed them.

Trees, many of them as round as he was tall were broken, branches were strewn about but being cut and stacked in neat cords. Who would use it, he'd not an idea but it was ready. And there was mud on everything. Not even their wagons had been saved from the things that had boiled out of the waters when the lady of the lake had lost her temper.

"Tell me again, if you please, what you heard when you said for me to run?" He knew of course but to see the look on her face when she told it. He would never forget the look, of course when she'd told him to run, his body tensing up for any and all manner of attack but to have water chase after you was something that he knew he could never raise his sword against and hope to win.

"I could hear it as you well know," Aurora said. That was something he really liked about the mistress. She could tell a story daily and it would still bring shivers to a grown man. He had no idea what some of the things were, that she described, but he loved the way she told it. "The breaking of the ice as it heated sounded like a freight train barreling down a track to its own demise. The scream of the water, just waiting to be shoved up and out of her confinement. When I realized we were going to be drenched, I also realized that the water was going to be hard, harder than stone when it hit us. My only thought was to save us from being crushed by some of the larger waves."

And large pieces of ice there were too. One such piece had been moved, with the help of the wings, to the front of several of the plots of gardens. As it melted, its water was giving back to the land it had once starved, he knew it 'twould be there for yet a few more days. Ox had explained to them that it was as pure as he could make it.

That had been enlightening to them all. Well, enlightening might have been the wrong word but it had been something. It had been all Trianam could do not to tremble in his boots when he spoke to them. The man...fish man had appeared to them just as the water reached its lofty brim.

"My lady," Ox had said to Aurora as they all bent on their knee before him. All of them with the exception of the champion herself. When he told them to rise, he put out his watery hand and started speaking. From the water. As water. "I am sorry this has come to pass. She would not be reasoned with."

"You didn't try all that hard either, did you?" the champion had demanded. Trianam had looked at Aurora wondering if she knew the power that the man had in just one hand. "You just had to make her so mad that her waters boiled up and came out, didn't you? Let me ask you something. No, let me make an observation. All men who are in power are just plain mean. Did it ever occur to you I might've been able to come to some understanding with her? Or did you think it was your way or the highway? Did it never occur to you what would happen to us when you made her so angry that she threw her frozen self at us? Heavy and hard self?"

"Nay, I only meant to help you—" Aurora cut him off.

"Nay, you meant to show off, show her that you were in charge. Ever think of bargaining with her? Maybe seeing what sort of deal you could make so it ended without the injury or death of so many trees?"

Trianam had made a mental note to ask her about this highway thing but he'd not found the...well, he was worried that she was still sort of out of sorts about the entire thing. It hadn't been her fault, the merfish had told her so but she still felt badly for it. He moved up to where she was using a bucket to pour the rainwater over the most muddy of places.

"Mistress, my I inquire as to why the others have not come to us from the North Village? The doorway has been opened for several days now and there has been no one, nor anything coming through to see what they might have missed." She didn't say anything for several seconds and he nearly walked away, thinking to ask her some other time. Her mood wasn't sour but she was quiet a bit more than usual.

"I'm afraid, if you want to know the truth. I don't know if it's a good thing or a bad one. Are they all dead? Or do they not care that we've opened this up? The village that we've just left, the South one, it had a damaged lake and an evil person impersonalizing me. Then let's not forget, we had a creature killing off the other animals in his area to make some money. I'm still trying to figure out how he was supposed to make that work." She stopped working and looked up at him. "Do they care, you think Trianam? Or are they dead?"

"I'm sure that we'll find out." They both stood there, neither of them saying anything as the sun beat down on them and the water pails between them sat unattended. There wasn't a sound. It was a sort of sadness here, without the chirping of the birds or call of an animal to break the silence.

Nary a bird flew overhead nor did a small animal, or for that matter, a large one come to nibble at the freshly grown foods they were planting. He could hear the men at the other end of the field they had cleaned just this morning, each of them with large baskets of vegetables they were picking and eating as they went.

They heard a shout and both of them went for their weapons. But relaxed a bit when they saw the woman coming toward them. It was forever an amazement to him when he saw the former champion. She looked young enough to be the sister of the current one in both looks and age. Yet he knew her to be much older than most beings that he'd met. Bowing low to her, he started off, telling Aurora that he had fishing to do for their sup.

Trianam had his pole ready when he felt the first tremor of the earth. Several days ago, just after the water had been filled in the lake, he'd felt a smaller one. Aurora had told him it was the earth settling around the water and that they were fine. Today, he looked around a little but didn't get over worried, until he felt it again. This time he stood up and looked around.

The first thing that struck him was the sound. It wasn't anything that he was familiar with, but he knew it wasn't something that he should be afraid of. His body was stiff. He heard something again and this time, he turned slowly in the direction it had come. The deer standing in the large field nearly had him dropping to his knees, his relief was so profound. Then he saw the monstrous stag come from the line of trees that they'd just planted this morn.

"They've only just arrived from the king," Zapps said. The stag raised his head from grazing and looked in their direction but didn't seem overly concerned so went back to eating as Zapps continued. "I was near one of the older trees when I was told to find the young mistress and have her put her boxes together. Lady Elizabeth came as well when I could not find her readily. I was on the other side of this world digging holes."

"He can do that?" He knew that he could send most anything through the portal, he'd done so earlier and it had saved their lives, he was sure. But to send a living being, that was something else altogether.

"From what he has told me, he was as unsure of it as you were. The stag, he volunteered firstly, and when he didn't die, his mates were sent through. I'm guessing we will have all manner of things soon." Trianam saw a flock of birds fly over his head. Then he heard the hum of bees. He watched as they made their flight to the fruit trees that were just beginning to open their delicate blossoms. Life, it seemed was coming to the garden after all.

As he stood there, Trianam thought of what he was seeing. A dead area coming to life. Not just that, but coming together as well, for more things to live here. Not just animals and plants, but people as well. He staggered slightly, his heart taking a hard pound when he realized that he had been a part of this.

"You are a good man, Knight to the King, Trianam the Warrior." The slap to his back nearly took him down. He turned to Zapps, to ask him to no longer call him names but his given one when he saw below him. If Zapps said anything more to him, he didn't hear him.

Trianam had thought her mad when she'd told him in the order that things needed to be put into the ground. Trees here, plants there. Even the flowers had a place in the way, whatever it had been at the time, he'd not seen it as he was now. There was order, color everywhere and it was laid out in a way that everything looked like it was a part of the previous plot.

Red flowers, he knew not the name of, from this distance bloomed just beside the pink of something else. Blue plants merged into purples and greens. Even the trees. The blossoms of the apples, startlingly white, were balanced nicely with the yellows of another. Bushes were beneath the trees, all of them looked as if they'd been there forever, their size and beauty a part of everything else seemed to yell at you to look here or look there. He found he wanted to see it all now. Not just see it, but inhale it into his body. Bring their beauty to him and let him feel what it would be like to have something so breathtaking around him.

"You will find me silly." Zapps told him he would not. "I know not how to describe what this is to me. To feel a part of something so large and something that will be here long after we have moved on. I can't tell you what this does to my spirt and my soul to know from the terrible we have seen, this can come out of it. Not just life, but 'tis enough but the beauty of it as well."

"You have described it very well, my friend. Very poetic, I think and apt for this work we have completed." Trianam asked Zapps if he really thought of him as his friend. "Now and forever, you are my friend, Trianam."

"And I you, as well. More than a friend, really. I would stand with you at my back and never worry that you'd fall to rest on me or leave me to be exposed when there is trouble about. You and the lady champion, you are, besides my brother, my family to my heart." He felt as if he needed to walk away and nearly did so, when he was pulled into a great hug from the troll. It was like being squeezed at his mother's washboard. There would be nary a drop left in him, should he have been a dirty rag left to be cleaned. When he was released, Trianam looked at the troll, then at the fields again. He found he needed just a moment, his emotions were getting the better of him. There were animals now, more than he'd seen a sometime.

"We will sup well tonight," Pavel said when he came to stand with them. "I've been sent to help you with the fishing. Aurora has said if you bring her a deer that she has spoken to, she will harm you in ways that you can't believe. I don't think she was jesting, either. She had that look in her eye. You know that one."

"Aye, I do. 'Tis the one she used on you last eve when you called a woman...what was it you called the women in your life?" Pavel told him. "Yes, that's the word. Do you suppose she knows that is what your females are called?"

"I don't believe she cared a wit about it. But I will tell you now, I will have a better care with my words from now on." They all laughed and readied their poles. Yes, they would eat well tonight. And have plenty to go around for seconds if any should desire it.

~~~

Aurora was full. Fuller than she'd been in a very long time. Lying back on her makeshift bed, she let the night's sounds, something so soothing now that she'd been without it for so long, that it nearly lulled her to sleep. The simple sounds of the woods were as comforting as the book in her hand.

As she drifted, her mind joining her body in the rest she needed, Illuminaria appeared before her. She was solid now, more so than Aurora had seen her before. When she smiled, it was as if the sun had blinded her momentarily, and she took a step back.

"The lady of the lake has spilled out her depths and something belongs to you," the queen said. Aurora wondered what it might be and must have spoken aloud, because Illuminaria answered her. "More of what you have. Something that will care for you in the coming months."

"Amour?" the queen nodded and sat down on the biggest chair Aurora had ever seen. "Your throne, I'm guessing. I had a thought when we were taking care of the castle that you might have one. I'm guessing that the king's is bigger still than this one. But I never saw one. Why is that?"

The laughter tugged at a memory long gone and Aurora tried to hold it this time. But the queen said her name, and she looked at her. Something she needed was there and she couldn't for the life of her bring it around to remembering.

"You will, when it's time. And as for this chair, it's his, my true and only love. As we spent more time in the sky, it came to be moved to the mountain," the queen said. Aurora found herself standing in front of the new lake, Hope they'd called it, and now she could see it for what it was. "I should like for you to return here on the morrow. Go to the place where the trees have new life and the grass is not yet formed. You will find a stone there, red as the blood that had been shed to make it so. Also, a blue one that is as dear to my heart as you have become," Illuminaria said.

"Go to the old trees where the grass is dead and find a red rock. Why must it always be so complicated when one of you guys tell me something? What if I were to say to you, go to the large new growth at the base of the mountainside and see what treasures are there. Don't touch them for they hold someone dear to my heart," she said. The queen laughed and Aurora felt silly. "I'm sorry. I guess it does seem different the way I talk to you as well."

"I'm happy that you have me close to your heart, Aurora of the New Dawn, Fighter and Champion of the Kingdom of Enneahedral." Aurora flushed hotly. They were forever calling her by names, adding ten or so titles to her name that would denote some greatness in her. "You don't feel you are a great warrior?" the queen asked.

"No. I feel like a person who has done what she could and hoped all of it comes out better. So far it's been good, but not all of it." Queen Illuminaria laughed again. "This part of my armory, what is it this time? And will I see it someday?" she asked.

"You don't know what you look like?" Aurora told her that there were no mirrors on the wagon nor had she found a bathroom that even flushed as yet. "We don't have either here, I'm afraid. I think when we opened the world things like that never came up. They had not been invented as yet."

"Well, I can tell you for a fact that a flushing toilet would be nice once in a while. And soft toilet paper." Aurora watched her face when she threw back her head in laughter. "The king will be so happy when you come to him. He misses you a great deal."

"And I him, but I don't yet know if I will be able to go to him. I know that I get stronger with every quest, but I don't know if that will mean he and I will be as man and wife again. I may be a specter for the rest of our days." Aurora didn't think so but said nothing. In actuality, she had a feeling that they were going to come together and she would be no longer any use to them. She would spend her days collecting money for making gardens winners of the —

"Aurora." Her thoughts dissipated when her name was spoken. "You are my friend, and Envir's as well, we will forever need you to keep us safe. There may be a time when you will be needed to help a garden along, but it won't be for a garden show. Besides, I do believe that would be cheating."

"More than likely." Aurora knew this was a dream, but to see the woman glide across the floor toward her had her wanting to kneel to her knee and pay homage. "You want me to go and find my armor, right? What else is there? I have a feeling that you're leading me on a merry chase and that I'm going to regret it."

"Nay, I would never lead you anywhere unsafe. I have had a thought to help you see yourself as I do. Close your eyes and I shall show you all you have been given." Aurora waited, not sure she wanted to see after all. "Please. I am...you should see yourself as I do. You will be most pleased with it. I have added the helmet you will get on the morrow, but the rest is you. All of you."

Closing her eyes, she thought of what she must look like. A woman play-acting at being a solider. Or worse yet, something out of those books were the woman was underdressed for the job and most of her body was too exposed for any kind of swordplay. Had she dressed like them, she was sure she would've been cut badly and not to mention how much Trianam and Karrah would have laughed at her.

Armor had been given to her by so many people now, even blades had been added to her list of war weaponry. The sword the king had made sure she'd gotten when she'd first arrived was as much as part of her dress now as her boots and shirt. But as the image of herself faded in, Aurora realized that she'd been wrong. Aurora looked as if she were readied for war, and her blue and red armor was fully over her body, covering her from head to toe. And she knew the names of them now. That had been in one of the books that the king had given her.

The breast plate she'd been given first from the queen was more than that. It was also the besagues, the part of the chest plate that covered her breasts and made to protect her armpits. It shone brightly in the light above her. Rerebrace also known as upper cannon, the armor that covered her from elbow to shoulder was there as well as the couter at her elbows, and the vambrace at her wrists and lower arms. Her hands were bare of the gauntlets that would serve to protect her from blades coming down on her own and the tasset, the skirt like part of her armor that hung over her hips was missing as well. She wondered briefly when she'd get it and from whom, but Aurora looked at the rest of her armor and was amazed at how well it fit.

Her leggings were covering her from thigh to foot. The cuisse covered her thighs, and the fan plate at the bend of her knees was there as well. The greaves and sabatons were over the lower part of her legs, the tops of the boot like metal was sharp and had several spikes at the heel of them as well as at the toe, looking vicious as well as amazing. The poleyns were dragons again, the design mimicked them in flight as they were on her treasure boxes. At the encouragement of her queen, she pulled the helm over her head as it hung suspended in air just above her head.

The visor with its eye openings were cut into the shape of dragons, one over each eye and in flight. She could see out of the holes they formed well and the gorget, the collar around her neck and attached somehow to the helm looked as if it were wings, flaring out from the sides to cover much more of her chest and shoulders. Lifting her arms up to see the rest of her, she noticed that nearly every piece of her uniform was in some way a part of a dragon, it's design worked into the hard surface to no doubt mark her as the champion of the king.

"I feel as though I should bow before you," the queen said. Aurora grinned behind the mask and thought she felt sort of royal, too. "You like your look? The way you appear as if you could do battle with any foe?"

"I do. I really do. I feel...it's incredibly light, isn't it? I had thought it would be so heavy that I'd not be able to move." The queen told her that it was because of the magic behind it. "Will I need such a gift, you think? Am I going to be in a positon that this will come in handy?"

"You have been using it all along, my champion. Every time you are hurt, the armor that you have on has kept you from being mortally wounded. You won't die now but you can be hurt in ways that make you wish you would." Aurora had thought that, even when someone had told her it had saved her life with the candel, she had a notion it had kept her from having a lot more damage done to her with the frozen king, too. "When you are fully dressed, everyone that meets you with harm in their heart will see you as I do now. Fully ready to do battle for your king. If need be, the armor won't just keep you safe, but those nearest you as well."

"Thank you for this gift. Not just allowing me to see myself, but to be able to guard myself against the people that try to hurt me and mine." The queen nodded and told her she must wake now. "No. please. I'd like to talk to you more."

Aurora opened her eyes again and found herself sitting on her bedding with the fire of the night just embers. Zapps and his cousin Tholan were there, they were playing a game of what appeared to be chess, and the rest of the men were sleeping around the fire. When the log popped to signal that more wood was needed, Tholan turned to take care of it, and saw her awake.

"My mistress, are you unwell?" she told him she was fine. "You have the look of someone that has seen a ghosty. You have not, have you?"

A quick glance at Zapps had her answering him so as not to scare the large man. She'd had to think on her feet several times so as not to give them *the willies*, as Pavel called it.

"No. Just a wild thought while I slept. Not a bad dream just... Tomorrow I need to go to the lake. I think I'd like to look around and see if there is anything we missed." They both nodded and Tholan went back to his turn but Zapps watched her before he spoke.

"Good thinking. I shall go with you, if you've not a mind." Aurora told Zapps that she'd like that. "We shall leave right after we have broken our fast and make a morning of walking the woods as well. There is all manner of animals out and about now and so we will need to step carefully, I think," Zapps said.

Lying back down, she thought of the conversation she'd had with Miss Beth earlier that night and realized that she'd forgotten to talk to Pavel. There were more than just the animals they had to look out for, but also someone who was out to hurt one of her men. A man who had a grudge against Pavel. The trees had told the earth and the earth had in turn told Miss Beth. It was the reason the trees had been looking for her today.

"The man seemed bent on killing the young lion and there is no reasoning with him. And no matter the amount of times he's been told it isn't a good idea, he is telling all who will listen to him that this thing, whatever it is, is the fault of Pavel's as much as his sire. The king and I are working to find what part of the kingdom he is in. This needs to end." Aurora had a feeling the only way it was going to end was badly for all. She wondered how the man thought to sneak up on a lion. Or even his human, or bear self. It was just too strange for words.

"You think he means to murder Pavel? Because of something that his father was supposed to have done centuries ago?" Miss Beth told her that is what she'd heard. "That's just nuts. What the heck does he think is going to happen when he tries to kill him? That Pavel will just let him? The man is a bear and a lion. There's no way he can hope to overcome either beast to kill him."

"Stranger things have happened. But the king wanted you to know. And he said you should, at all costs, not let him harm you or your men." Miss Beth snorted. "Like you would let that happen anyway. There are times when that man makes me wonder if he'd not been dropped on his head a few times too many. Let them hurt you indeed."

And now she had to figure out a way to tell Pavel, and make sure that they were all ready. For a man that no one knew what he looked like, here to kill a man that could become two different animals and in a place that no one could tell her. Yes, things were going to be so easy with this one.

CHAPTER 9

Zapps watched for the man. There didn't seem to be a way he could be here, not as yet he thought, but watch for him he did. The lady champion had told them all this morn about him and Pavel was to be with someone at all times. Zapps thought this was good idea but Pavel was less than thrilled, as they'd all heard the champion said on occasion. She moved to stand near him as they were closer to the dense trees that had not been harmed by the lake. He didn't blame her in this; the woods were a scary place to even him at times.

"I'm guessing that Tholan doesn't know we speak to the queen," Aurora said. He said he didn't, and Zapps thought it best that few people knew it. "The way she just pops in and out, its small wonder that the king isn't aware of it. I wonder what will happen when we're all at the mountain," she said.

"No one sees her as you do. I do because of our bond, but others, the people who talk with her and see her, they only see what they want. Knowing that the queen is dead, they don't see her when she walks among them. They see a woman who is only our friend." The champion said nothing and he had to smile. He loved to see her working out a problem and coming to the right decision. "My lady, what is it we are here for, if you don't mind me asking."

"A piece to my armor. She said it's here. She told me that the lake had it. But when it emptied out, she came to me and told me it was here in the woods." He nodded and wondered if the champion knew how dressed she was. Then he realized that if the queen told her what was to come, she might know by now. He asked her about it. "Yes. I saw it last night in a dream. At least, I think that's what I saw. It's really fancy and beautiful."

Not a word he would have used to describe the way she looked to him. Warrior like, yes. Even medieval as well. Strong and courageous to be sure. But fancy? Not really.

He wasn't sure what she was looking for until they found the red stone. The stone, a ruby, if he was correct was lying beneath another stone of brilliant lapis. Zapps had a little thought that perhaps the champion might not know what they were supposed to be until she picked them both up and put them together. He nearly fell back when the vision before them made itself known. It was his first view of his home in this form.

"It's the tapestry." He nodded unable to talk around his surprise. "I've never seen it like this. All brightly done and without some of the borders like this one is. The one and only time I had it, it was dull and frayed a little. The dragon in the middle was alone as well."

The areas that the champion had been to were completed. Their colors were bright, as if the stitching had only just been put to cloth. When the magic had been breached at the castle and the king had gone to rest, the lines in the tapestry had closed off. Now the areas including the trees and animals were all about the place.

Even the gardens, where they were now, the lake was a peaceful blue, the grounds showed their bounty as if they were showing off.

The places they were yet to go, the North Village and the rest were there, their colors bright but not as much as the ones that were completed. There were people milling about, almost as if they had not a care they were stitched in the fabric of their livelihood. He even saw smoke curling softly out of their chimneys, looking as real as he was standing there watching it. He could swear he could smell what simmered over it, almost taste, actually.

"Do you suppose this is telling us what we have yet to fix? Our quest is there, if we only look hard enough?" He didn't know and said as much. "I wonder if I could touch it. See if the horse that looks in motion would feel like he's slick with sweat and winded."

He didn't want to tell her no, not to touch it, for he wanted to know as well. But he had a feeling that as soon as they tried to do such a thing, it would be forever gone to them. When she sighed heavily, he knew she was going to take the stones apart and the view, the lovely vista would be gone. And as surely as she'd pulled a blanket over the sun, the image disappeared when the stones were separated. His sadness was profound, his heart ached a little to no longer see what he was sure no one save the two of them had ever seen before.

"I guess we should look for what I came here to find," the champion said. He nodded, eyeing the stones as she put them in her large satchel. "I don't think we should tell them what we've found, do you?" she asked.

"Nay, I don't, my lady." She nodded and turned her back to him, but not before seeing her sadness.

The helmet was right were the stones had been. Sitting there, in all its glory like it had been there all along. As soon as she put her finger to it, touched only the mane of spikes that ran down the length of it, it like the other armory appeared on her body. Zapps was amazed at what the piece did for her appearance.

"Can you see the armor on me?" He nodded still, thinking about the tapestry, but also the sight she made dressed thusly. "Are there really dragons at my eyes, and on my breast plate? Do the poleyns, are they decorated like dragons? One blue and one red?"

"Yes my lady." He found himself wondering when she got to the king, if he'd give her the sword that had been hanging above the mouth of his mountain for so long as he'd known him. It was all her amour needed to make her look the part she was doing, the sword of Enneahedral. "You are most impressive standing there like you are. I wonder should a beast come upon you that he doesn't run in the other direction crying for his mother."

She flushed and Zapps smiled. As they made their way back down to the encampment, he wondered what else would befall them as they moved to the next panel on the great world. When she spoke, he had to have her repeat herself, as he'd been trying to think what else could go wrong for them.

"I said the doorway opened at both ends. By the time we get to the wagons, there will be any number of others coming to see us. I wonder what sort of treats will be there for us when we arrive." She had other things on her mind, he knew from the way her voice sounded. He wanted to ask if mayhap they could rest for a bit longer, but she would not and he knew that the king wanted them to come to them. He also wondered what her tool had been. There had been no people here to go on with them.

There were indeed some of their friends there. Trianam was there, holding his child, a fat little boy with cheeks as red as the hair upon the champion's head. The babe's mother, lady wife to the knight stood there, holding her tears back as she watched husband and child reunite. Even Venitice was there, his wife fat with child too. Also the young miss and her dolls, so many that she had her daddy fashion her a cart to carry them in.

Mykaal was set to come on the morrow, his children with him. And a new wife as well. Sophiand had a child now, his father as proud of him as he could ever have been. Karrah held them both in his arms as they sat together and there wasn't a better looking couple, Zapps thought. Even the witch had come, her wagons full to the brim with more soaps and herbs. Medicines to give them as well as more seeds. The rest, they were told were to come with young Mykaal.

A sheep was brought in for their dinner and all manner of things to go with it. Fish had been caught by the dozens, the vegetables of some of the plants were also brought forth and cooked on long fires set up to feed them all. Zapps wandered over to his mother and aunt and sat with them and Tholan. He had missed her more than he could say.

"I have a small gift for the champion. And something to give to you as well." His mother handed him a small package that would look so much bigger in the hands of the champion. "You will see that she gets it for me. I've no desire to see her when she opens it. I have...she is very dear to my heart, she is."

"I will make sure that she does." He opened his own package and smiled at his mom. "You are getting very good at this. I will be the envy of every troll that we meet." He pulled out the beautiful vest that she'd made for him, and wondered aloud if Aurora was getting the same thing.

"Nay, she needs what I have made for her. Better boots for one, and socks. I have a nice pattern I have put to parchment that I made. I think she will like it." Zapps told her he was certain she would. "I do have a wonderment, my son. What will you do when this is over? I've a mind to spend some time bouncing children, grandchildren on my knees."

"You have another child that I don't know about that is to be wed?" She smacked him soundly on the arm. "I don't have a desire to settle as yet. And there is much to do before I can leave her. You know that, as well as I do."

"I do. But a mother can hope, can she not?" He kissed her on her cheek. "I do so love you, Zapps. And the girl. She has given so much of herself that I can't believe how much it has not changed her."

"Changed her? How do you suppose it would change her?" he asked.

She seemed to be thinking of her answer, and he looked at the champion now to see what his mother meant. She was much stronger than she'd been so many months ago. Her hair was longer and now in a constant queue at the back of her head. At times she wore it under her shirt but he rarely saw it down about her shoulders. There had been a point when he'd thought her too thin but she looked fit, her body like her mind, grew stronger with each passing quest. He looked at his mother now.

"'Tis the magic I think. She doesn't let it go to her head as most would. Even when she uses it without thinking, she does it so gently...so nicely that I doubt that she knows herself that she does so." He was watching Aurora, now and saw a cup just out of her reach come toward her. Her conversation with the good lady Sophiand never pausing. His mother was right, she didn't know she was using it he would bet. "And then there is the way she has you men working with her. Not *for her* as would be the case in most places, but together as a team."

"I love working for her." his mother told him he didn't work for her but with her. "There is little difference in what you say, Mom. She is our leader, and we work for her."

"Nay, son. You don't. You work together for a common cause, and she is the one you turn to, but I believe that she turns to each of you when necessary." He thought she was right on that as well and told her so. "You must learn, I'm right in most things but I don't rub in into your face. I am, like the champion, gentle in my ways," Mom said.

Zapps couldn't help it, he laughed. It earned him a good smack to the back of the head, but he laughed still. Kissing his mother when he could no longer sit with her without causing harm to himself, he moved to stand near the wagon the witch had brought. It was his turn to guard it anyway.

~~~

The doorway was open for Aurora to pass though, and unlike the time before, she had no desire to go alone. She needed them, her group of merry men as much as she needed to eat or sleep. When Karrah came to sit beside her as she thought about passing over, she watched him with suspicion. He was a man she'd never felt she could be herself with. There was too much...she supposed it would be because he was so warrior like. Stupid, she supposed but that was it. He could slice her in two she knew as well. Maybe she'd be able to hurt him now, too, but he still intimidated her.

"Do you have a moment? Can I ask you a favor?" he asked. She told him that she'd do most anything for him. "I was hoping you'd say that. On the morrow, Mykaal and his family will come here and I've...I should like for you to turn him down."

"Turn him down about what?" He told her. "You think he wishes to go with me? To the new area? And you want me to tell him he can't go. Why? I thought he had the orchards to take care of."

"He has it in his head he is no longer needed there, because the men and women who work for him have it under control. His children have begged him to stay, as has his new missus. I would ask that you turn him away." His smile made her think he thought it was a done deal. But it didn't work that way. "It's a small thing I ask of you," Karrah pleaded.

"I'm sorry, but I can't do that." He nodded and started to speak. "No, you don't understand. I have no control over who goes or stays. I'm only the one that moved forward in this thing that I know has a purpose. Trianam is my tool, as you know as are Markard and Vildar. Before it was Zapps. His cousin came along but I'm not really sure why the walls allowed him and not others but I don't get to pick. If he comes with me, it will be because the magic allows it. And if you let me be honest with you, I will tell you that I think you're wrong for asking me to do something so cruel."

"Cruel? You don't think it cruel to leave his family without him?" She said nothing as he seemed to be gearing up for a nasty snit. "You wish for his new wife to be alone without him to protect her? That he move through this world and mayhap get himself killed. What would she do then, I ask you."

"You'd leave her to the wolves, Karrah? You'd not raise your sword to help her if she was left alone?" He looked shocked. "I know you would never do such a thing, and even if Mykaal were there, she still might need you. But, you must remember, had it not been for him, I'd be dead. Had he not taken me under his wing and helped me to understand what I was doing, I would not have gotten as far as I have. His family clothed me, fed me when I had nothing to give them in return. His mother stitched me clothing out of her own to make sure that I was warm and dry. If anyone should be allowed to go with me, it would be him. And him alone. So, no, I won't tell him he can't go. And I'm hurt that you would think that I would."

She stood to leave him, her hurt and that was what it was, was deep and profound. He grabbed her arm and she looked down at him. "I meant you no harm, my lady. Had I thought of all of what you have said to me...well, I would not have asked. I should not have asked something like this of you. I beg your forgiveness."

"He's my friend." Karrah nodded and she sat back down. "Does he really want to come with me? I can't think why. It's not all that much fun and it's stressful. And besides, we need him here to bring me news and seeds."

"Aye, 'tis stressful for us too. Not knowing what has befallen you. You've no doubt of that. But I think he feels as if he could be doing more." She asked him why he'd feel that way. "The orchards supply enough foodstuffs now that we are able to have all the pantries full. A shop, under his supervision has opened, and wares, not just the fruit from the king's trees, are traded but gardens in the village as well. People are eating better than we have in many a year. There is friendships now that there was never before. He has even put up an internet."

"Internet?" Her mind went all over the place with that. Cell service here? How was that even possible? Before she could ask him what kind of phones he was offering, Karrah continued. "At first we thought him mad. Putting up this large net in the village square. And there were parchments there as well. Stacks and stacks of them in a large basket. It's said he'd gathered the papers from rubbish piles and from his own home. The first thing that was put there was a notice to say there would be a town meeting. The time was there as with the date. Then a second one was put up. Someone needed a roof, could they get some help. It was answered in a few days and she now has a roof. More and more notices went up. Need of a help with canning. One man asked for a tree to be removed from his yard and that the wood would be free to whomever took it down. You would not believe what Mykaal had accomplished with this internet." She could well imagine

She couldn't help it. Aurora started to laugh. Then when it became apparent that he was confused, the look on his face made her laugh all the harder. It took her a good ten minutes of trying to calm her laughter to tell him what was so funny. Even then, Karrah looked completely confused by it.

"It's nothing. Just something he and I talked about so long ago that I'd completely forgotten about it." Karrah nodded. "He's a good man, our Mykaal. A very good man. And I'm proud to call him my friend."

Hours later she was still laughing about the internet. It was a brilliant idea. He'd created his own sort of search engine and it was working well for the community. Aurora was going to have him help anyone interested to set one up in the different areas. She had a feeling that Venitice would be very receptive of the idea as well. But for now she had work to do.

The plants they'd planted were coming along nicely. Some of the people from the castle had come and started helping with the harvest. And Genese had some other seeds that they were putting in the ground when it started to rain again. She supposed that it was necessary, but Aurora had had enough water and cold to last her some time now. But the plants, like the trees were needed to keep the ever circle of life going.

"There be some things I've been playing with whilst you've been playing at work." She turned and ran to Mykaal and hugged him tightly when he put his arms out to her. "Aye, my lady, I have missed you greatly as well."

"You got married." He nodded and introduced her to his lady wife. He told her that they were expecting and asked if Aurora could tell them what they were to have. Cara was beautiful and just beginning to look like she was pregnant and she smiled when Aurora agreed. Aurora put her hand on Cara's firm belly and smiled at the woman. "It's twins, did you know that? Both boys."

"I've had a feeling, mistress, that there was more than one. Should have guessed, meself being one of twins." Aurora nodded and told her they were both healthy and strong. "Like their sire. We have been so happy these last months. The older ones, they call me momma already," Cara said.

"As they should." Mykaal left them to get the bags of seeds he had, and Cara and her moved to the shelter of the trees. She could tell that Cara had something on her mind and was ready to ask her when the king spoke to her.

"*Should you be dallying?*" Aurora told him to hush up. "*I have it in my head that you are coming to see me. Silly me. Here you are having meals with friends and sitting about on your bottom as if you've nothing better to do. Is this how you repay me for all that I've done for you?*" the king said.

"*I don't, really, have anything better to do at the moment I mean. I'm...you're not going to mess up my good time today, so hush up.*" He laughed. "*Why are you bothering me today, anyway? I have my family here and like you said, we'll be having a nice sup. Is there something pressing? Did you need for me to tell you how a plane flies? I don't know in the event you are asking me,*" Aurora told him.

"*Nay. I wish only to let you have fun. But I can feel your worry and would like to see what it was about. You are doing well, my champion.*" She thanked him as she looked out over the vast fields. "*I can't wait to see the gardens again. It will be a sight to behold once you have finished all the quests set before you.*" the king said.

"*I think it's coming along nicely.*" Aurora thought about the vision she'd had just had. "*I would like to ask you about the man that comes for Pavel. What can you tell me about him?*"

"*I know nothing more than he has been saying for months now, nay, years that his family has been slighted in some way by Pavel's family. His father, Xander, was a good man and by all accounts, fair. Whatever this man has in his head, he thinks Pavel must pay for, I can't find it.*" She asked him if there was any word on where he might be as well as what he might look like. "*Nay, I know nothing of the man other than he has been holding onto this grudge as if it were a treasure to him. I would think that it...never mind. I should like to know when you meet up with him. Please be extra careful, as we are yet unaware as to where he is and what sort of tricks he might have up his sleeve should he find you. I would...I have no idea if he has a weapon or even if he can use it,"* the king said.

"Me either. And so you know, the things that you sent us, what was left over has been distributed to the people here. All the mittens and other blankets too. I don't know when winter will come again here, because the seasons are really messed up, but they can use them. From what I understand, the North Village won't be cold, correct?" He told her that he didn't think the gardens would have been either. *"I guess not. We leave tomorrow, just so you know. And since I've no idea what we'll encounter or who, I will close tonight with hopes of talking to you tomorrow when we cross over. As you have pointed out, I have a supper to eat,"* Aurora said.

"I don't wish for him to go." Aurora had forgotten about Cara as she talked to the king. Sitting down on the other stump, she asked her what she meant. "Mykaal. He wishes to go with you when you part here. I don't wish for him to go."

"Have you told him this?" Aurora asked. She shook her head. "Then I would suggest you do it and soon. I leave in the morning, and if the wall accepts him, he'll not be able to return until that quest, whatever it is, has been finished."

"He will speak with you about it. I fear that you will tell him yes." Aurora told her what she'd told Karrah. "I'm glad that you won't tell him nay but I still worry for him to be gone. With the babes on the way, I should like for him to be here."

They both looked up when they heard Mykaal whistling. The man could do so and not have a single tune in his head, yet it still sounded good. As he got closer, Aurora could see he was worried about something and asked him about the bags of seeds until he was ready to talk about it. His wife went to have a lie down and see to the other children and he walked with her to where some of the others were still gathering some of the garden's bounty.

"They think I wish to go with you and be a part of this grand adventure." Aurora said nothing, not even sure what to tell him or even to ask at this point. "I do wish to go, but I know I can't. I have responsibilities that require me to stay behind."

"You do. But you should also know, you are on the adventures with me," Aurora said. He laughed. "No, you really are. Every seed I plant, every tree that comes up, is because of you and your talent. When I put a hole in the ground and fill it, you are there with me. Every time we pull a piece of fruit from a tree or a vegetable from the ground, it's you I think of. We would not be here, not like we are without you there with us, Mykaal. You are the reason that the gardens are now a garden again. So in a way, you are more important to this quest thing than most of the people who come with me. If we didn't have the seeds, we'd be leaving the garden in poor shape as well as all the other places that we've been, too."

"You humble me, my lady." She smacked him on the arm and laughed with him. "I feel...I need more to do, I think. I know that I am to be a father again, with two more sons. My other children, they are growing so fast, they no longer need me to be their gentle reminder. I can't even care for my mother now, as she is happily married with her own home and hearth. I feel...I know there is more I can be doing. But I feel at a loss as to what it might be."

"I was going to talk to you about that. I was wondering if you and your family would stay a few days after I'm gone to help set up the internet you have at your village. Karrah said that it's working very well." Aurora said. He flushed brightly. "Also, Venitice said his shops aren't doing as well as he'd hoped. There is money...coin but they are hording it rather than using it to keep the shops open. I think they might have it in their heads the castle might fall to ruin again and then what will they do."

"I think he does need a stable there as well." She asked him why he thought so. "Most people don't wish to walk to the store or to have to carry their things home. I have set up a merchants carry service that will deliver items to those who can't walk far or are in need of some help. Even people are being conveyed back and forth, for a coin. I believe it's why we are doing so well. There are more people about than before. I have even...we are expanding to the South Village in a few weeks so that we might have some of their wares brought to our village. They have a place that has a loom and cloth of many colors."

"That's brilliant. You're very good at this. Please, talk to Venitice and Nizel, when he comes in a few days. He is helping run the South Village and the pasture as well." He said that he would. And Mykaal asked her if he might set up someone in the pasture to help with that as well. "You do what you need to do to make this work. I don't know how you'd do that sort of thing here, there are very few beings around, but I'm sure that you'll get it worked out."

By evening meal Mykaal was having meetings. Several at once at times, people were coming in to get ideas and to listen to the ones that he had. Venitice had even suggested that they set up a nice house for learning, so most if not all his people could not read or write. As she went to bed that night, Aurora put her hands into the earth. Not to ask for help in keeping them safe, but to give more of herself in order to make the new plans happen.

CHAPTER 10

This wall they were to cross over was dark. Forbidding actually. As they stood there, their wagons loaded up and water barrels cleaned out and refilled, she wondered what sort of thing they'd find here. She was almost afraid to look and see. But knew as surely as she was standing there thinking about it, the thing wasn't getting done. Three more panels and she'd be with the king.

This move was going with a different kind of tool too. She looked over at the large empty wagon. Aurora had been told it could be filled with things, like more seeds and trees but she had a feeling it needed to be empty. Its purpose was for it to carry something around and to be full when they crossed over would defeat the purpose of bringing it. She had no idea what it might be needed for but only knew that it had to be empty of everything. When Trianam stood beside her, his sword drawn, she did as well.

"Are ye ready, my lady?" She nodded. "Then we should go. I've a mind to get back sooner rather than later. I've a bigger family to get to know."

"You could stay." He told her she could as well. "Yeah, and have that annoying voice in my head yammering all the time to get my butt in gear? No thanks. I'll get this done and go to the closest beach I can find and lay on it for the rest of my life."

"Aye, that is a plan, I suppose. Then what will you do ten minutes after you have your lay about?" Laughing with him, they nodded and stepped through the large wall.

"Trianam?" he said he was there. "What...where are we?"

"I know not my lady." She could hear the fear in his voice. "Get to ready," he demanded.

All of them stood hard and fast. There was...she had no idea what they were looking at but it wasn't a village. There was...nothing. Not a void but everything had been destroyed. Burned to the ground, the embers still smoking, it was so recent. Trees were toppled over, house, or what was left of them were in ruin.

"What happened do you think?" Aurora asked.

No one said a word as they moved forward. That was when the smell touched her nose. "Someone...something is dead," she whispered.

"Aye. I see them." Them. Not it or even a he or she but them. As they moved forward more, the wagon, the one that had to remain empty moved along with them. "'Tis a ghastly mess. We'll need to work quickly so that we get them to rest."

Yes. Fast. The smell and the heat would not do well to make their task any less monstrous. As she and Trianam put their swords away, the rest of the men stood ready to protect them as they moved forward. The two of them began shifting through the rubble to seek anyone alive.

The bodies, seven so far, were loaded in the wagon to be taken somewhere for burial. They'd been in bed, all of them. The grate in the fireplace was the hottest place and they both figured that it had begun there. The house, it was a large one Trianam told her, with two stories, had more than likely filled with smoke and had overcome the large family. She surmised there were three children and four adults. It looked like a husband and wife, children, and two elderly women. All dead.

"How do we tell who they are?" She didn't expect an answer and got none. Someone needed to be told this family had not survived. "Pavel, set up a search party to see what you can find. There might be...I hope not, but there might be more houses like this one."

As he moved off, Pob with him, and Tholan, she looked around. There wasn't a garden in the field, something that tugged at her mind. Nor were there any animals, not even a cow in the barn that had been burnt too. She wondered if there might have been a spark from the house, but Trianam never answered her as he wrapped up one of the children.

"They've been killed, my lady." She moved to where he was working and saw that he was right. The child had been killed then set in her bed. "Who would do such a thing to someone so small? There is no reason for this to be as so," he said.

Before she could answer him, two men rode up on horses. She watched them move around before her and Trianam moved toward them. Even their wings, with their bodies tall and spread out, moved to stand just behind them. Nerves were tense and she didn't want anyone else to get hurt today.

"What have you done?" She looked behind her at the house then back at the man who'd spoken. "You have murdered that family for no good reason whatsoever. You will pay for this."

His knife came out quickly and Aurora didn't have to look to see that her men had drawn their swords as well. She stood there, with her feet braced and her arms crossed over her chest, glaring at the man.

"We only just arrived here. And I'm pretty sure you know that, as we're strangers to you." the man kept his knife held out toward her. "Do you really think you're going to get close enough to me to use that? Or for that matter, to even get off your horse alive?"

The other man just sat on his horse, and said nothing. The horses were getting nervous, she could tell. The wings, all of them, had surrounded the men and it didn't look like this was going to end well. Pavel moved to stand beside her and she glanced at him when she heard him clear his throat.

"You know who these people are?" Aurora asked.

The man that had not spoken earlier, said. "The Sampsons."

"Do they have kin about? We can take them to them so that they can be properly put to rest."

"You'll do nothing of the kind. That is the mayor of our town and we take care of our own." Aurora looked at the knife welding man then at the other one when he laughed. He turned to look at the man laughing. "You won't think this funny if they were to go about murdering us all in our own beds."

"They did nothing here but to bring them some peace." The second man looked at her. "You are her, are you not? The one they say will bring us peace."

"You need peace here?" he pointed to the grisly scene behind her. "I take it this is not the first time someone has been burned from their homes and left to die."

"Nay, they are the first to be burned this way. Usually there is a hanging for a small infractions. Or a drowning. That was the way things were taken care of until the lake was set with guards." Aurora was going to have a talk with the lake when this was done. "You are the first to come here in a long while, my lady. So I ask again, are you her?"

"Yes. I'm the champion of the king. Aurora Kirkpatrick. And these are my merry men. To harm them is to harm the king, and I will make sure you pay." She looked pointedly at the man with the knife. "You use that and I will cut you to ribbons, my good man. I'm in no mood to screw around with you today."

"I am Lord Frodaka and this buffoon is Vilan, the self-appointed sheriff of this town." Vilan took offense to the man's words and turned to him. But Frodaka just simply told him to shut up. "We are in need of someone like you, to my way of thinking."

She wanted to like the man, Frodaka, but didn't let her guard down. There were people like him all over the place. Say they were your friend only to cut you apart at the first chance they got. As she told him what they'd found, Vilan finally put his knife away and started to help them put the poor people in the wagon to be taken to their family.

"You do not trust me." She said nothing to Frodaka. "I shall have to work harder to make it so that you do," the lord said.

"It won't matter, really. I make my own decisions." He nodded and closed the back of the wagon when it was loaded. "My men and I will bed here for the night. We'll head into whatever you have as a town in the morning."

"You will." She didn't understand what he meant by that but said nothing. "I should like to shake your hand," Frodaka said.

"I don't think so," Aurora said. But before she could back from him, he grabbed her hand and pulled her to him. The pain of his tight grip was nothing compared to the pain she received from the touch of his hand to hers.

Now available in
The Kingdom of Enneahedral Series

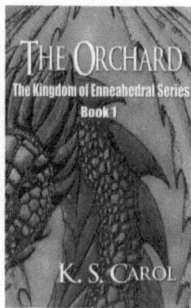

The Orchard
The Kingdom of Enneahedral
Series Book 1

The Pasture
The Kingdom of Enneahedral
Series Book 2

The South Village
The Kingdom of Enneahedral
Series Book 3

The Castle
The Kingdom of Enneahedral
Series Book 4

ABOUT THE AUTHOR

I have a story to tell. Some will say it's a very vivid tale from a very strange author. Others will tell you that I should be locked up, that things like this just aren't true. But they are.

The story I want to tell you really happened. How do I know? Well, I was there. The dragon king, Envir gave me permission to come back from his world and told me to tell the story so that others, people like the ones in the story will know there is hope.

I will tell you my name is K. S. Carol. I'm not...not really. But for the purpose of this book that's who I'll be. I'm a teller of tales and the scribe of my world. Not this one, but one that defies all that you have known.

Aurora was having a bad day. Actually she was having a bad life. Her mother had just died and she inherited a tapestry, a knife and a box. But she didn't want them. She wanted her well ordered life to go on well ordered. But the Lady Elizabeth and Envir decided that things would be better if she came to them. So when she was trying to decide what to do with these new gifts she fell into the beautiful tapestry.

Her life as she'd known it was gone. The world in which she found herself in was rich in magic, creatures she'd never heard of and a few she thought only to be myth. Aurora was their only hope and she thought that with her...

Well, it would be very unfair of me to tell you the whole of her story before I've begun the tale now wouldn't it?

www.ingramcontent.com/pod-product-compliance
Lightning Source LLC
Chambersburg PA
CBHW051944170626
46808CB00007B/2475